Hardcover: 979-8-9888013-2-0

E-book: 979-8-9888013-1-3

Paperback: 979-8-9888013-0-6

First Edition

Library of Congress Control Number: 2023914398

Rickeydlyfe@gmail.com

Young Kaz

So I woke up one morning listening to the song *That Makes Me Feel Like I'm On Top of The World* by R Kelly. The title of the song was *"The World's Greatest."* I was nineteen years old, just learning about life and what it had to offer, not knowing that I hadn't even begun to live or learn the true meaning of life.

"Kaz! Hurry your ass up, boy. It's time to go to school. You only got ten minutes," Mom shouted.

I can't lie, sometimes I just wanted to scream out loud and say, "Leave me the hell alone, Ma. Can't you see I'm fucking tired?" but I knew how that would end—me passing through a football line with her in front followed by my uncles and aunties, waiting to give me the beatdown of my life. So that thought went out the window quickly.

As I was going to school, I saw this tall dude with muscles, fresh from top to bottom. I thought to myself, *Yeah, when I get older, that's how I'm going to look*, but coming back to reality, I didn't even know how to work out or how I was going to make money to buy clothes. I was wearing sneakers my mom made to school while everyone else was dapper down. Anyhow, this tall, buff dude had this girl in his arms, and I swear, she looked like a beautiful black model.

"Hey! Get out of the street, you little shit!"

I replied, "Fuck you! Punk!" and ran to school, which was only a block away from my house.

"Ok, Kaz! You know the routine."

"Come on, Ms. Williams. I'm late! Can't you just let me in?"

"Now you know I would, but my job is on the line, and you know how that is, right?"

Yes, I do.

I attempted to run straight in, but not fast enough to be serious. "Come on, Ms. Williams. I was just playing. I wanted to see if you still got it," I said jokingly.

"Now come on, Kaz, you know I'm fast! You lucky I like you."

If only Ms. Williams really knew why I made her run after me. I always seemed to stop right in time to catch her breasts bouncing in the air. Well, another day in this hellhole... Science class was so fucking boring.

"Mr. Armstrong, I'm here. Sorry I'm late, but my mom made me late again."

"Have a seat."

I wasn't sure how long I could use that line, but it worked. Man, why was this seat always hot? No one should have been sitting in my seat. While class was in session, I was still thinking about Ms. Williams and her breasts. I wondered if they were soft or firm and how her nipples looked. The table slammed with a thick book, scaring the shit out of me.

Rickey Dudley

I was late for class.

"You come in here late! This is the fourth time, and you do the same thing! I will not tolerate it. If you don't want to learn, don't come to my class."

"Mr. Armstrong, that's why I'm here, to learn all about science." Truthfully, I didn't care about school, but I couldn't tell him that because the only thing that would happen was my mom would come into school, speak with him, and beat my butt in front of the class. And I didn't want that.

"Kaz, why do you drift into a daze every time I speak to you?"

"The truth, Mr. Armstrong? I was just thinking about the stars. Why does everyone say that they're planets? Planets don't move!"

"Kaz, you never cease to amaze me, but we're not on that topic today. Perhaps we will discuss that another time. Now stay here on Earth so we can get this work done."

I tell you, Mr. Armstrong always fell for some crazy science talk. Once again, if it works, don't stop—that was my motto.

The bell rang again. Best time of the day—gym time! I raced to my locker room to change and return to the court where everyone was, and I squatted on the bench to lace my sneakers. Wait a minute!

I'd never seen her before... *Oooh my!* What size breasts did she have? Now I knew it was not only me that saw this girl. And wow, her kitty looked fat! I would have loved to smell in between her thighs.

"Let's go, Kaz. I'm going to break that ass off something proper!" says Ceto. Little did he know, that was what I was thinking about with this new girl.

"You ain't busting nobody's ass over here, boy! I'm like Jordan in the air. Pass the rock!" I told him.

Yeah! That's how I'll do it. I'll let her see how nice I am on the court. While getting up, I realized I was rock hard. I'd made a big scene bringing attention to myself by yelling in the gym at Ceto. Everyone continued to stare my way. Oh well, I couldn't sit back down now, and thanks to Ceto passing the basketball like he was on the football team, making me hustle hard to catch the ball, he forced me to show my receiving skills before it went out of bounds.

Let's just say the ball wasn't the only thing bouncing up. I think it worked because I saw all the females gathering, pointing, and smiling at me while I showed this random kid my skills. He knew he couldn't guard me; I gave him an "E" for effort.

Young Kaz

A quick game to five was all I needed to show off. *Is it me, or did I see Ms. Williams eyeballing me on the low?* "Kaz, pass the rock! Oh yes! Never mind, get 'em, boy!" "That's all you. Take him straight to the whole."

That's my boy, Ceto. Ceto was this Spanish cat I met when I first got to school. Some punks tried to jump me; I guess they thought I was a punk. Ceto saw that I could hold my own and still jumped in to help me fight off those bullies. Shit, sometimes I asked myself, "How the hell did he get a crazy ass name like that?" I'd never heard of a Spanish cat by that name. Ceto was short with green eyes and a mini curly flat top, had a medium build, and was fast on his feet. I didn't play too long because I just wanted to get a little attention from the ladies, and I got what I wanted, so I was off to the locker room.

"Yo, Ceto! I'm out, kid. Maybe next time we run a full court."

"Really, bro?" Shit, that was a good game. I really did want to stay, but gym time was like 45 mins, and it was almost over. Time sure did go quickly when you're having fun, and besides, that was not even enough time to enjoy a full court.

What the hell! Ms. Williams was walking toward me! "Ms. Williams."

"Kaz."

Damn, she just walked past me like that. I guess she didn't see my long black crowbar. It was swinging like it had a mind of its own. *What would it be like to have a one-night stand with Ms. Williams?* Hold on! Was it me, or did I hear loud, sweet music in my ears coming from the hallway? Yeah, buddy! It was, but one of those voices sounded familiar. Oh yes! It was on! A moment to remember for the rest of my life. "Ok, get it together, Kaz. Come up with something," I tell myself.

I wondered if I walked out just like this with my shorts still on… *Oh yeah, let me get my crowbar up so I can be hard as a rock.* Shit, if I jerked just a little bit, I could get hard before they passed the locker room. Damn, this feels good! Batter up, and here they came—fuck it! I was going for it. Out the locker room with a hard-on and no shirt—yeah, they were going to feel me, and I got my chest pumped up. It was on.

What the fuck! Right when I came out of the locker room, I bumped into the old janitor lady with a hard-on. The crazy part, she was bending over to pick something up. Not only that, but the girls saw me ram right into her. Dammit!

"Papi, be careful with that!" the lady replied.

"I'm so sorry I didn't see you."

"It's ok, Papi!"

Hold on, was it me, or was she smiling? *What happened to that beautiful melody with the girls talking?* I thought to myself. Then I heard, "Yeah, Papi! Be careful with that!" from the girls, sounding off as they departed.

It didn't go according to plan, but the end game still hit home with the girls. I just wanted them to get another good look at me with my shirt off and my crowbar. I went back into the locker room to retrieve my belongings and head home. *What! Is this janitor lady telling on me?* All I saw was her talking to Ms. Williams. *Here we go!* I said to myself, hoping the janitor lady was not telling on me. I really didn't mean to bump into her from behind like that!

As I walked past her and Ms. Williams, all I heard was, "Mommy, please! Make sure you lock that door because I see many kids leaving there after hours when it should be closed." That was a close one!

"Ok, Kaz! Have a good day, and make sure you don't come to school late tomorrow!" Ms. Williams replied.

"Okay, Ms. Williams, have a good day." You would think the janitor lady would say bye as well, but I guessed she was upset with me. Then again, I never really saw her speaking to anyone unless they were in her way while she was working or speaking with security. That was fine by me; it just meant everything was back to normal. Another day in the neighborhood, at least they could've cleaned the streets while we were in school.

Out of nowhere, this old man cries out to me, "Hey, you little shit, get out the damn street!"

"Fuck you, grandpa! One of these days, I'm going to fuck you up!" I replied while running.

I had to stop daydreaming like this, especially when crossing the street. Anyhow, I was back home at last in my room, just kicking back on my bed, looking up at the ceiling and the posters I put on my wall of D.M.X, Jay Z, and 50 Cent. There were a few others along with my black power leaders, such as Malcolm X and Marques Garvey—you get the point. I was just thinking, *Damn, I would love to have their lifestyles. They can pretty much get anything they want. They have the money to do so.*

"Kaz, I need you to go to the store for me, get some white flour, half a gallon of milk, and butter," Mom yelled. I hadn't even settled in yet, and she wanted me to go right back out. Sometimes I thought she was a psychic. It was like she knew what I was about to say or think. "Your ass wants to eat right. I don't see you moving!" *What was it with this woman?* I thought. How the hell did she see me moving when I was in my room?

"I heard you, Ma! I'm getting ready now!" I replied before she had another outburst.

Young Kaz

Make sure the butter is margarine, and the flour is Aunt Jemima."

"I know, Ma, I know!"

"Go to the store, go here, go there…" I mumbled to myself.

Man, I tell you, I couldn't wait until I got older. I'd just hire a maid to do all that stuff. As I was walking to the store, I saw Ms. Williams closing the gate to the school. *That's odd.* She was in her regular clothes and not her uniform! Goddamn! What a woman. Ms. Williams pushing that BMW, no way! The school was not paying her that much.

"Oh shit! Stand tall. Here she comes," I said. I could feel my palms getting sweaty.

"Hey, Kaz! What are you doing over here?"

"Hey, Ms. Williams, I'm just going to the store for my mom to get some things."

"Aww, that's cute! So, you must live in the area?"

"Yes, I live one block away from the school. Why are you over here? What were you doing in school? I thought you were supposed to be home by now?" I asked.

"I had to stay late because of the aftercare center. Well, you take care, Kaz. I have to go."

"Ok, see you later."

Wow, what a woman! I needed her in my life when I got older. Then I heard that damn voice again, "Hey," and before that voice could finish, I said, "Fuck you!"

"Excuse me, young man?" the police officer replied.

"Oh shit!"

"What did you just say to me? You're a very disrespectful young man. You need to learn some manners."

"I mean, excuse me, Mr. Officer! I apologize for my response. I'm just having a bad day!"

"It's ok, young man. Just be careful crossing the street. There are sick people out here that would run you over and wouldn't think twice about it."

"Ok, have a good day, officer."

As I was walking away, I burst out laughing to myself. I can't lie, I was scared to death. While I was finishing up getting the items for Mom and heading back home, I started thinking about Ms. Williams. That woman looked amazing!

"Kaz, put the stuff up for me. That's for breakfast in the morning. When you are ready, your food is in the microwave. The juice is in the fridge."

"Ok, Ma!"

Now this is what I'm talking about—fried chicken, mac & cheese, spinach, and biscuits! Yeah, buddy! While scarfing my food,

I couldn't stop thinking about the new girl from school. She kept popping into my mind; I could still see her sweet smile with those tight gray sweats riding up her booty.

This week was boring. I didn't have any fun in class, thanks to my dickhead science teacher... Fucking fart face! But it's cool. I know he's just doing his job.

Rickey Dudley

"Thanks for the food, ma! It was delicious!" I said while going to my room. After a while, I fell sound asleep.

It was a beautiful morning! Today was the day I got to see the beautiful girl that had been racing through my mind. The crazy part was, I had no name to go with that beautiful face, but I'd find out today. I was already walking out before my mom could even knock on my room door.

"What the hell has gotten into you this morning?"

"Nothing, Ma! I just want to get my education in today. What's wrong with that?"

"Ok, mister. I just thought you wanted to get an edjumacation."

"Wow, Ma! I didn't know you spoke Ebonics."

"I used to be young and hip back in my day! I used to drop it like it's hot, had the boys going crazy over my ice cream."

"Stop it, Ma!" My mom may have had a little too much coffee this morning, but that was why I loved my mom. She was crazy and funny at the same damn time. I believe she was wild in her teen days.

"Stop, Ma! That's nasty! I have to get ready for school." I was laughing to myself while Mom kept dancing as if music was playing. Sometimes she made my day better before it started. But man, if you thought she was too much, you should've seen my pops! He swore up and down that he was the true macaroni, may he Rest in Peace. Knowing him, he's probably chasing the girls wherever he's at. Man, that guy was my everything. When he and my mom got together…oh boy! It was a headache, but at the same time, you were going to have a blast around them. They always had jokes about one another. If you weren't up to par hanging with them, the jokes would be on you. No exception, kids included. If I ever fall in love, I want my relationship to be like Mom and Dad's.

"Ma! I'm heading out to school now."

"Ok, baby. Enjoy!"

While walking to school, so many thoughts were racing through my mind. I couldn't focus; I was thinking about the roads to becoming successful and what the key was to having all the women in the world. I could hear my pop's voice saying, "Son, don't try to please every woman that you meet because some women are not meant to be pleased. On another note, women are like Skittles— you never know what color you're going to get. The colors represent their attitudes. And son, remember, the most important thing is that most women belong to me!"

"Oh my god, Kaz! Come here quickly!" said Ms. Williams, interrupting my thoughts.

Not understanding why she was calling me with such urgency, I rushed to her aid. "Ms. Williams! What's wrong?"

Young Kaz

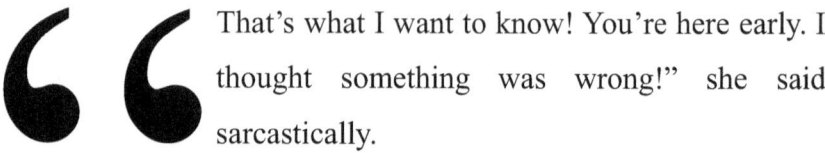That's what I want to know! You're here early. I thought something was wrong!" she said sarcastically.

"Oh! You got jokes! I'm doing well, just got things on my mind."

"Ok, I'm here if you need to talk."

"Cool, talk to you later." She smelled amazing!

"Ayo! Kaz!"

"Damn, bro! Why do you have to yell? I'm right here."

"Let's go to the bathroom. I got something to show you."

While walking to the restroom, I was just wondering what the hell Ceto was up to now. "Yo, check this out, man!" said Ceto.

There he held the "Holy Grail." The answers to the exam! How in the hell! Truthfully, I didn't care how he got them. I was just glad he had them, not to mention I didn't study for the exam.

"My guy! I need a copy, bro! My life is on the line here. I need to pass. If I don't, that's my ass," I pleaded.

"Calmate, papa! This is your copy. I told you I got you."

"See, that's why I fuck with you!"

"You only fuck with me because you know I got all the girls," Ceto said. We both laughed, but I knew he was lying like hell about the girls. Still, I played along. "All right, bro, you good. I'll holla at you later."

"Hold up! Where are you going?" I asked, curious to know.

"I bagged this little cutie, and I'm going to pick her up now. I'll kick it with you later."

"Ight! Playboy!" I replied.

Time couldn't have flown by any faster; it was already gym time, but I didn't see her. I wondered if she was in the female locker getting ready for me. I had that type of effect on females. *Yeah, I know I'm full of myself!* Ok, Kaz! Man up. I heard the female's voices, so here they came…

Fuck me! No, this couldn't be happening to me! *No! No! No!* I shouted inside. I kicked back into my player mode, nonchalant. Here came this fine girl I'd been dying to see since last week, different sweats, but they fit the same. Camel toe looked amazing. I felt like a happy dog looking at her. But I had to suppress my happiness because I was boiling inside, watching her smile in Ceto's arms.

"Kaz, what's good, bro? This is my girl, Nadine. Nadine, this is my brother Kaz."

"Hey! Nice to meet you," I said with a bit of jealousy.

"Ok, enough of that. Time to get that ass beat in some ball, kid."

I wanted to play—truthfully, I did—but my heart was broken. It was not Ceto's fault because he didn't know I wanted her. The only thing now was to just take this loss. Besides, I couldn't just sit here and watch him kiss and touch her like he was now.

"Nah, I'm ok, bro. Not into playing right now. My head is bothering me, so I'm going to hit the locker room. I'll get up with you later. Take care, Nadine," I said, feeling sad.

Rickey Dudley

I can't lie, my boy Ceto had taste. He probably used one of my lines to pick her up.

Nothing like a twenty-minute cold shower to cool me down. Damn, I needed that.

I knew I wasn't bugging, I wasn't that thirsty for pussy, but did I hear a female in heat? "What the fuck!" Ok, me and Ceto were the only ones that knew about this low-key spot where we could investigate the female's locker room from this peephole we found, and yes, that was exactly where I heard that noise coming from.

I couldn't believe my fucking eyes! My bro Ceto was eating shorty out. Man, her moaning sounds were beautiful—she had my bone hard as hell. I don't think my shit ever got that hard. *Damn, I got to bust this one out.*

Now this was weird because as I started stroking myself to bust this mean nut, watching Ceto eating shorty out, he started looking right where our peephole spot was set up. He leaned to the side like an acrobat with the tongue still in action. It was like he knew I was there to watch. Yes, sir, I was! Damn, she had a pretty little phat pussy.

"Yeah, Ceto, tear that shit up!" I said to myself. I must have sent him a telepathic message because he threw the ok sign up as if he heard me. He then started lifting her shirt! "Oh my fucking god!"

Look at those titties. Now I was really feeling a little bad because I would have loved to be in his shoes right then. I couldn't take any more of this! Ceto was about to put his bone in her, and I didn't want to see his shit. Party over for me. To my surprise, I turned around, and the janitor lady was standing right there, not saying a word, just looking at me.

"I can explain!" I said nervously.

"I would like to hear this one!" she said.

"What had happened was—"

Before I could utter another word, she just went in on me in Spanish. I had no clue what she was saying until she spoke in English. "Papi, what the hell are you doing in here?!"

I could see it now, me being labeled as a pervert and getting suspended once the principal found out. *How do I explain this to my mom?* I thought.

Then she speaks in English and says, "Papi, that's no good. You are setting up here, spying on the females next door, standing here butt-ass naked. How do you explain this?"

"Yes, I know! I'm so sorry!" Then it came to me. My pops always said, "*It will be worse if you lie. Just tell the truth.*" "Well, you're right, but I've never been with a female before, and I heard some moaning, so I just came over here to where I saw a hole in the wall to see what was going on. I really don't do stuff like this. Honestly, I don't. I won't do it again! May I ask you a question?

21

"Pregunteme, Papi."

"I don't speak Spanish," I said, reminding her.

Young Kaz

"Answer me, Papi!"

"What are you doing in here, anyway? It's not time for you to clean in here, so I guess we both are in trouble."

Maybe I went too far because she was getting close to me like she wanted to swing at me. *Please don't let this lady lose her cool, God, because I will hurt her if she puts her hands on me*, I pleaded internally.

Her hands reached out, grabbing my dick instead. *Oh lord, her hands are so soft. I feel like I'm about to melt.* She started speaking to me in Spanish. *Oh man, I don't know what she is saying, but it's making me hard again.* Then she said, "Papi! You like? Don't tell nobody, okay, or we both would really get in trouble."

I could barely talk, but somehow, I just managed to say, "Yes, Mommy!" I closed my eyes in disbelief. I felt her tongue circling the tip of my dick. *Oh my god! This feels amazing!* I thought. I then felt something tight and warm.

Is my dick really inside this grown woman? I ponder. I had to see for myself. I did a Kevin Hart one-eye peek, just to be sure. I was wrong—she was sucking my dick so slowly. My dumb ass forgot that I was standing on the chair—that's how good it was. I just closed my eyes and enjoyed the moment.

"Papi, look at me," she said. I was under her spell. Somehow I burst out, "Ceto!" In my mind, I'm like, *You are not the only one getting busy.*

I replied to her, sounding tongue-tied. "Yes, Mommy! I am looking at you."

"Papi, talk to me! Tell me you like."

" Yes, Mommy. I love you! I mean, I like you! Damn, I mean, I like it." What the hell just happened? I could barely talk, but I guess she found it funny because she started laughing with my dick in her mouth. This was the best day ever, I swear. "Mommy, can you put it inside?" as I point toward her camel toe.

"No, Papi. You too young!" "Okay, Mommy."

"Don't worry, Papi. I'll take care of you."

I must have said something magical because she started going crazy on me.

This experience was inscribable but imagine electrical impulses sending waves of dopamine to your brain.

"I'm about to…"

Before I could say "come," she replied, "Ahora, Papi!" Shit, I knew what that meant, thanks to Ceto. I had to let loose before she changed her mind. What I couldn't wrap my head around was that she said *now*! My shit was still inside her mouth. Maybe she knew that she would move when I was about to come.

I giggled to myself, knowing that I busted hard.

Rickey Dudley

Ahora."

The next thing I knew, I felt that tingling feeling. I realized this was it! I was about to have my first nut without jerking off!

Mommy didn't budge at all; she held her post down. She swallowed every drop from me, and my legs began to shake uncontrollably as if I was about to transform. I felt like I was about to fall flat on my face, as all my energy had zapped out. I sat down for a while as if I was on time-out.

"You taste good! Don't tell nobody, ok? It's our little secret."

"Ok, Mommy, I won't," I confirmed.

Now, you know better than that! I couldn't keep this secret, I just had to tell Ceto, but I started second-guessing it. If I told Ceto and she found out, I might not get to put my bone inside her, and we both might get into trouble. Yup! My mouth was sealed.

"See you later, Papi!"

"Yes, Mommy. See you later!" I almost forgot where I was and most definitely forgot about Ceto bagging Nadine. It was time to put the clothes on and head out. Here came Ceto, racing like a madman into the locker room.

"What the fuck was that about?" Ceto said, sounding like a madman. I smiled but paused because his posture was different. It was more on the aggressive side, and I was wondering what happened. I quickly forgot what he was talking about because I was so excited about what had just happened to me. I couldn't wait to tell him.

"Fuck you talking about, bro?" I replied.

"Now you want to play dumb. You dead to me, Papi," he said with anger.

"Here we go again with this Spanish shit! And what the fuck is it with all Spanish people calling everybody Papi? Though I admit, it sounds good coming from y'all women!" I told him in a joking manner, not taking him seriously.

"You don't even care! I thought we were bros!" he said in a sad tone.

"Oh, shit! Nah, we are bros, but I have no clue what you're talking about."

"So, I'm eating her out, right? That's when I looked up, hoping you were watching. That's why I threw the ok sign up."

As he explained, I was getting excited for him and cheering him on as if I didn't see it. "Yeah, yeah!"

"Then I pulled my monster out, and she was ready, bro. Wet like crazy. I was going to put it in, and then I heard a lady say, 'What the hell are you doing here?' I jumped up because I thought we were busted. The loud noise went away, and I had to start from scratch just to get her back in the mood. When I finally got her back in the mood so I could lay the pipe down, I got three good strokes in, and then I heard your voice, "Ceto!" and she pushed me off her. I got dressed. She didn't even help me get out of the female locker room. That's how mad she was."

Young Kaz

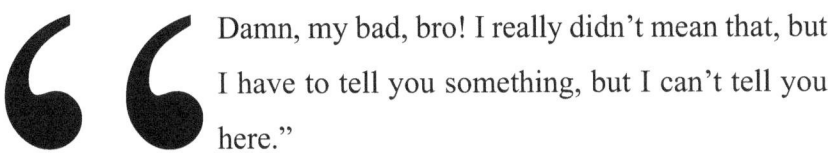Damn, my bad, bro! I really didn't mean that, but I have to tell you something, but I can't tell you here."

I was so excited to tell him what had happened to me, but the look on his face had me on guard. "Ok, bro," he says with a smirk, not being able to keep his madman face.

"You're smiling! So that means we are good, right?"

"Fuck you, bro! Hell no. I'm mad. I'm mad I couldn't get what you got, punk. I'm still the number one player, thooooough."

"Hold up! What are you talking about?"

"It's not hard to tell. I speak Spanish. I heard her. "Ahora, Papi!" We both bust out laughing. Damn, this was really the best day ever. My best friend was not mad anymore, and we both scored. I knew deep inside he was pissed he couldn't finish up with Nadine, but he would get over it. Then it occurred to me that I kept my word, but the janitor lady was going to think I told.

"Yo, Ceto! Bro, you can't tell anyone. She told me not to tell and if someone else finds out."

"Calmate, Papi, calm down! Relax, bro, the only one that knows is me, and I'm not going to say anything."

That was a sign of relief, but I still hoped he didn't. "Tell me, Papi, how did you do it?"

"Do what?"

28

"How did you get her to do that to you? I know you were speaking like me." I really couldn't come out and tell him the truth; it seemed too far fetch, so I just kept it simple.

"I can't even explain how it happened, bro. It all happened so quickly."

"It's cool, but you know if I was there, Papi, she would've never even looked at you. I'm the real McCoy. The true Papi chulo."

"Yeah, okay, Ceto. Hail to the true Papi chulo, Ceto!"

Today was a good day for me. Unfortunately, it wasn't what I had in mind. I really wanted the new girl, but it is what it is. Now the whole time I was getting my things and talking with Ceto, this older lady had my mind going crazy. I was asking myself questions about her and answering them myself, not really paying attention to what Ceto was saying. The only thing that came out of my mouth was, "Yup, you're right. I'm down with that."

I really didn't hear what he was talking about or what he had asked. I agreed and said I was with it. Right after, he walked away. Hold up, what the hell did I just agree to?

Ceto was my boy and all, but that was one crazy dude. I remember back in the day, he got in trouble for pissing on the teacher's seat. I think when God made Ceto, he got distracted and must have put Ceto's brain in upside down. Here's what I mean: I was not a criminal expert, but if you had committed a crime, you would run because you didn't want to get caught, right, or didn't want to get caught? Well, Ceto, being a genius, waited for the teacher to come out of the school, then busted the teacher's car window and ran away. He was special, that kid.

Rickey Dudley

While walking into my house, my mind was distracted by seeing my mom with some dude dancing in the middle of the room. I didn't know what it was, but I started boiling inside. Truthfully, he caught me off guard. The door slammed shut behind me.

He turned around quickly, and at the same time, my mom replied, "Boy, what the hell is wrong with you, slamming my damn door like you run shit."

"Oh, I didn't know there was a man in the house. Pardon my manners," this stranger said.

I had never been addressed that way before. I guess that calmed me down, but I still wanted answers from my mother on why there was a man in the house and was puzzled at this stranger's response.

"You want to explain yourself, Ma, and tell me why there is a stranger in the house?" Suddenly I felt like Jodie from the movie "Babyboy" starring Tyrese, except this guy was going to get fucked up, messing with me.

"First thing first, this is not your house. Do you pay the bills? Hell no. So take your ass to your room that I pay for and calm yourself down, then come back out here like you have some fucking sense and start over before I lose my cool."

Before I proceeded to take a step toward them, he spoke, "Now I know that's your son, but he's right. He deserves as much respect to know. After all, he is the man of the house. Now if you may excuse me, I have to go to the store. Anyone want anything?"

I looked back at him like he was crazy for even looking my way, but at the same time, I gained a little bit of respect for him. "Nah, I'm good, thanks," I replied.

"I'm okay, honey," Mom responded with a smile full of lust. As he was leaving, I watched my mother as she replied. The only time I'd seen her talk or even light up like that was when she was with my dad. I looked at him to double-check to see if I was missing anything, but the door closed.

As I turned to look at my mom, I saw her open hand aiming at my head. I dodged her one-hitter quitter and ran into my room, laughing to myself.

"I'm going get you back, punk!" Mom shouted as she laughed. I played soft music and just lay on my bed, looking up at the ceiling, thinking about the janitor lady.

Young Kaz

What possessed her to do something like that? She couldn't have been that thirsty. How many other kids had she done this to anyway? *Life is great*, I thought to myself, and then I heard a knock at the door.

"Yo, Kaz, it's me, Marvin. Can I come in?" Now what the fuck did he want?

"Yeah, come in."

"Hey, I just want to apologize for coming into your house without your permission. Your mom told me she had a son but didn't say you were a grown man."

"I'm still a kid, man."

"Yes, you are, but you're the only man in this house, so in my eyes, you're a man, and you're going to protect your mom by any means, am I right?"

"Yes, you are! I'm willing to kill for her if anybody tries to hurt her, too." I made sure to make that clear to him so he knew that if he hurt my mom, I was coming for him.

"My point exactly. That's how I am with my mom." This guy was not bad. He had respect—that one I'd give him. "Ok, now that I got that out the way, can you come to eat with us? That's if you don't mind me being at the table. Your mom had cooked my favorite fried chicken, mac and cheese."

"It's cool, but maybe next time." This dude… Mom must have told him I loved mac and cheese. Maybe she told him for a way to get on my good side. *Sorry, dude, it's not working, but I'll give him an A for effort.* As he walked out the door, it dawned on me that this guy would never hurt my mom. He might just be a good fit, but I'd have to adjust to this guy being with my mom. Being that my pops passed away, I have no choice. After all, I do want to see my mom happy. I would just have to eat a little bit of mac and cheese first. As I made my way to the kitchen to get some mac and cheese, I heard them laughing up a storm. After noticing they were kissing like Eskimos, I disregarded them and headed straight for the mac and cheese that was almost gone. Damn, I guess Duke wasn't playing when he said it was his favorite; he must really be a mac-man like me.

"I see someone changed their mind. Don't worry, I left the rest for you."

I was about to myself, *Dude, I'm a man. This is a plate for a little baby,* but right before I could finish my sentence in my head, he replied, "There is more in the oven. I asked your mom to make an extra pan for you just in case you changed your mind. Besides, men eat big meals, not baby meals."

"Right?" I said.

As I agreed, my mom looked my way in amazement, seeing that Marvin and I were connecting on some level.

"Ok, big man, I'll call you when it's ready."

As I made my way back to my bedroom, I figured if I was going to call myself a man, I might as well look and carry myself as such.

Rickey Dudley

A definition of a man to me is having a Ronnie Colman body with a Malcolm X mentality. I started doing some pushups and sit-ups to complement my handsomeness. Unfortunately, I couldn't do many, thanks to the janitor lady sucking the energy out of me—literally. So I just kicked back and waited for the mac and cheese to finish. About five minutes had passed when my mom called for me. Yeah, buddy!

"Kaz, come and get it." I wanted to run out there like a pit bull, but being a man in all—also to impress Marvin—I just strolled out to the kitchen. But to my surprise, he was gone.

"You can stop showing off now."

"What do you mean, Ma?"

"I see you putting on for Marvin. He's not here—he left." My mom knew me better than I knew myself, but I still carried on like I had no clue what she was talking about. She was right, of course. The only thing she was wrong about today was this plate she made for me. I could eat a cow with the way I was feeling.

"Slow down and stop eating like a pig. You're eating like someone sucked the energy out of you." I looked at her and paused for a split second. "Good thing I made a lot. The rest is in the oven."

"Thanks, Ma."

"That's my baby! Let Mama taste the chicken. I cooked it differently this time." I suddenly had a flashback of the janitor lady sucking all my energy, and knowing that she was someone's mom, I quickly thought about how all women must have done that sometime in their life—there was no way I was going to let my mom use my fork. You could say I had been traumatized now.

"Come on, Ma. There's more in the oven! I'm really hungry."

"Well, excuse me, big man. I will get my own." She snatched a piece anyway, but the chicken was cooked so well that it fell off the bone and on the floor. "Dammit, someone wanted that piece," she replied.

"Yeah, me!" We both laughed. After I finished my food, I couldn't help but ask that question. "Mom, what is it that women want from men?"

"I knew it. I knew it!"

"What are you talking about? You knew what?"

"My baby got a girl on his mind!"

"I'm a man, Ma! I'm not a baby anymore, and she is not a girl. I got a woman on my mind, Ma."

"Ok, a woman. Y'all kids grow up so quick nowadays." Truthfully, my mom had no clue it was a grown woman that I was talking about.

Young Kaz

"Yes, Ma. I just want to be a gentleman for the ladies—a real lady's man."

"Yeah, sounds like being a player to me."

"Ma!"

"Ok, I'll tell you this much, some women like to be played with, but they're not going to tell you that's what they want. They love the drama of cheating. You have to understand that it's part of the game."

"Played with… What do you mean by that?"

"Some women like to be treated like they are God's gift to the world, and then you have the ones that have no respect for themselves. They will sleep with any Tom, Dick, or Harry just to say they had him. You know, the female version of a male player."

"That means they are sluts, then, right?"

"No, baby, you see, those types of girls are like men. They think and act like men by trying to fuck everything that moves. When you see those types of girls, run. They will mess up a happy home just to prove a point—that some men are dogs. In some cases, they do tend to be right at times. Now you've got the pretty girl type that loves her man and will do anything to please her man. All she wants to do is make her man happy!"

38

"Ok, so I know to look for a pretty girl?"

"Now, hold on, baby. Just because a girl is pretty doesn't mean she's a good one. Sometimes those are the ones with the most problems. They think they are too damn good to do anything. On the other hand, you got a woman like me—I'm a bad chick! All the men can't control themselves when I come around. Trina ain't got shit on me!"

"Ok, Ma!" She laughed, cracking herself up. "Then you've got the funny girls." Mom started doing dance moves without any music playing, doing the pee-wee Herman and the running man.

"I'm done, Ma. It's my bedtime," I said. My mom could get silly sometimes, but that was why most men fell in love with her.

"Thanks for the chat, Ma. Goodnight."

"Goodnight, baby. Oh, Kaz! Do you really like Marvin? It's been a long time since I've been with someone besides your father. I love your father, but he's no longer here, and I feel empty being alone. I tried my best to find someone like your father or at least someone I thought you would like!"

As I looked back at her, I saw how into Marvin she was, but it was my approval she was waiting for. "Yes, Mom, you did good. I think I can get along with him. It's just going to take time."

"Not too long now because he's moving in tomorrow."

"Come on, Ma!"

"I'm just kidding, baby, but we are having that conversation soon. Get ready for school tomorrow. Love you, goodnight."

"Ok, Ma."

Mom was a real jokester. I was going to bed satisfied with a full belly. Yeah, buddy! I was good, and now it was time to get some rest. I had a big day tomorrow. I closed my eyes, and it didn't take long before I fell into a deep sleep.

Rickey Dudley

The crazy part was I knew I was asleep, but the dream felt so real. Within seconds, a beautiful woman appeared right in front of me. She was a beautiful black woman, her hair in a powderpuff afro style, with a nice silky black dress. Her breasts were almost the size of cantaloupes, with her nipples shooting straight at me. She was coming straight toward me. *Ok, control yourself—you got this.*

"Hello!" My voice quivered. "My name is Kaz. What's yours?"

"Star!" she replied in a nice voice. "My name is Star! What can I do for you? I'm here to please you in any way."

"Is that right? You know I'm only nineteen years old, right?

"And if I told you I was eighteen, would that be a problem?"

"No way. I just wanted to let you know that I'm young. Because you look older—I mean, not as in bad old but a good older beautiful woman that only dates older men."

"So, are you telling me you're not a man?"

I was nervous as hell. This woman intimidated me; her body was thick in all the right places, looking like a grown woman.

"Calm down, baby. I'm not going to bite unless you want me to, and yes, I'm twenty-five years old."

"Wow, you look beautiful for twenty-five, Ms. Star."

"Well, have you been with a woman before?"

"Yes and no."

"Silly. It can only be one answer."

I said no, keeping my oath to the janitor lady by not telling her, but I had to say yes. I didn't want to look corny in front of her.

"Why are you so nervous?"

"I don't know."

"Well, what did you and that grown woman do?"

"She kissed me."

"Like this!?" She leaned in and put her lips on mine.

"Wow, no, she kissed me down there!" I pointed down to my private area. For some strange reason, I felt like I would be disrespecting her if I just came out and said she sucked my dick, so I put some respect in my conversation with her.

"Like this?" Hold up, was I really going through with this again? Oh lord, her hands were in my pants! She began stroking me, and then she was getting on her knees. Ceto wouldn't believe me on this one. Oh man, it felt just like with the janitor lady.

"Oh my god, Star. What did I do to deserve this?"

"Why, don't you like it? I'll stop."

"No, please keep going!"

"That's all y'all did?"

"No, she finished me off!"

"You mean she swallowed your sperm?"

I figured, why not just tell her? She might just do the same thing.

"How about I do something better than that?"

"Like what?" I replied.

Then she rose to her feet, taking a couple of steps back and pulling down her dress. I just stared at her. "Oops, can you please help me put my dress back on?"

I was so nervous I rushed to pull her dress up, but she grabbed my hands. *Oh, man.* "Ok, before you pull that dress all the way up, let's get on this bed." *Now where the fuck did this bed come from? This shit is weird.* I still couldn't believe this grown woman was here doing this with me. "Now, I want you to do these motions with your middle finger. Rub that little button, which is my clit, softly, then in a circular motion. After that, slide that middle finger down slowly until it falls into a hole." Wow, I couldn't believe I was doing this! "Yes, baby, just like that. You like the way that feels?"

"Not really."

"Ok, stand up, baby, and pull your pants down."

Oh god, I'd been waiting for this moment for the longest, but this was a grown woman. *I might be making a mistake*, I thought. I always thought my first would be with someone my age.

"Don't be scared, baby. Do the same thing I showed you with your finger."

"Ooh, yeah! Daddy, just like that."

43

What the fuck? Ok, so I got it now. The Spanish woman said *Papi* and the black woman said *daddy*. I wondered what Chinese women said. *Stay focused*, I told myself. "Do it like this, then like that."

I asked, "Did I do something wrong?"

"No, Daddy, you're doing fine. You got it, just like that. Go ahead, Daddy. Push in now. Not too hard, ok, because are you going to hurt me."

Oh my god, I did just what she told me to do, and here went that little bit of thrust to be inside her. Oh my, there was a heaven. She must have felt what I felt because she made the sweetest sound. She began to moan, and every time I pumped inside her, she moaned even harder. "Faster, Daddy, faster. Now harder, baby, harder. Now switch it up, baby, and go as slow as you can."

"Yes! I'm about to come. Hold on."

"No, Daddy. Come in me. This is all yours."

I tried not to, but it felt so good I didn't want to stop pumping. Aww fuck it, here it comes.

As I continued to pump, she continued to moan, and then I began moaning too. It was so good that she kept calling me Daddy, and I started calling her Mommy. She hit my butt every time I pushed in.

"Ok, Mommy, here I come." The bad part was that while I was screaming *Mommy*, I woke up to my mom spanking me on my butt to wake me up for school.

Rickey Dudley

"Aww, my big baby is calling for his mommy. Someone having a bad dream? Get up, big man. It's time for school."

"Ok, Ma. I'm up." Oh my god, what the hell just happened? After Mom closed the door, I quickly threw the covers off me to find that I had a mean hard-on, and my underwear was wet and covered with sperm. Well, I guess that was what a wet dream felt like. Now, that was amazing! I felt like I had a 101 lesson on sex.

"Ok, baby. You are getting close to that time."

"I know, Ma. I'm clocking the time!"

I get up to handle my normal hygiene routine before leaving the house. On my way to school, I noticed the attention of some girls. Some of them started looking back at me as if they knew what was going on in my mind. This girl here looked beautiful! While soaking up the moment, admiring the beautiful woman, I heard that rude, nasty voice again. "This fucking kid. You make my day a living hell! Get the fuck out of the street."

Being that my week had been ok, I wasn't even going to respond. I'd just move out of his way even though I really feel like cursing his ass out, but that would be a waste of my time. The only thing on my mind as I walked across the street and into my school was what would go down today.

"Good morning, Kaz. Nice to see that you are taking school seriously," said Ms. Williams.

"Yes, I am. I have a couple of things I would like to do when I get older."

"That's good to know. You are heading in the right direction. I saw a couple of my old friends from high school, but one still comes to mind, June-bug. His real name was June, but we gave him the nickname June-bug. He never stayed in school—he would cut class just to chase women. It got so bad that he started asking some of the girls he used to date to help him fill out job applications. He couldn't read."

"What's wrong with that?"

"He couldn't read, baby. That's a big no-no! Real women want a smart man with a job or his own business, you know, doing something with yourself! That's how you get all the good women. June-bug got caught up in the system. I saw him last year, and he's homeless now."

"Yeah, you're right. It's time for me to get to class now. See you later, Ms. Williams, and thanks for the chat."

"Have a good day now, young man." Just that quickly, you could learn about life and how it could change in the blink of an eye if you listened to older people when they spoke. I paid attention to elders a lot when they spoke, which helped me become wise. I soaked up as much as I could when listening to Ms. Williams. After all, I was young, not dumb.

Young Kaz

My goal in life was to become someone of importance as I got older and to bag good-looking women. Honestly, I came to school to bug out and have fun, but that lesson Ms. Williams put me on to had opened my eyes in another way.

When I heard about June-bug, I said to myself, "Oh no, not me. I always said that I would never depend on anyone or become homeless. Don't get confused, I wasn't too proud to seek help if I needed it. My schoolwork was first. I wanted to be able to read and be a smart man, so as of this day forward, I was going to stay focused and be serious." But before I could get the "serious" out of my mouth, who came into the room, clowning around? Ceto's crazy ass came in singing, "Don't stop, pop that booty. Let me see you do the Brown!" and dancing at the same time. Now you know I did my best not to laugh, but I couldn't help it. This dude had me and the whole classroom in tears.

"Ceto, either you calm yourself down or get out of my classroom with that foolishness," Ms. Blue shouted.

"Sorry, Ms. Blue! I was in the moment. I thought I would cheer you up because you're blue. Doesn't that mean sad or down or something?"

"Sientate, ahora." Ceto came my way, and I was still in tears trying to keep cool.

"Fool, you going with me to get some burritos at McDonald's?"

"You know you that special new type of stupid, right? You got me in tears, bro," I said while wiping my tears away.

"You know me, bro, I like to live life and have fun. You remember when I told you I had something? I brought it with me for after the bell rings. Let's go to the locker room or the bathroom. As a matter of fact, the bathroom is a good spot. The teachers won't come in there as they have their own restroom."

"Slow down, bro. I don't remember anything like that."

"Damn, bro. You said you were with it. That's why I looked out for you and got you your own joint."

"My own joint?"

"Yeah, that's what's up." At the same time, I told myself, *This dude is on some freaky shit. How the hell is he going to get these girls in the bathroom?*

We had fifteen minutes left on the clock before the bell rang. As time passed, I just kicked back, watching the females and admiring their beauty. When we were down to one minute, me and Ceto got our bookbags and stood by the door. In less than a second, the bell rang.

Rickey Dudley

"Kaz, let's take our bags and put them in the locker room first." Instead, I threw my bookbag on the bench beside my locker.

"I'm ready, bro!"

"Copy that. We out!" So as Ceto and I left the locker room, we walked the halls as if we owned them. I looked at Ceto, and he looked like he was ready to kill someone, and of course, you know I had to look at my reflection in a mirror somewhere, so my swag got off track a little. I then caught my reflection in a mirror on one of the classroom doors.

"Yeah, boy, I'm pimping heavy, you heard," I told Ceto, feeling myself.

"Papi, you ready?"

"Check you out. Am I ready? This is what I do."

Ceto dug into his pocket and pulled out two joints. *Oh shit, what the hell is going on here?* I said to myself. *Yeah, you really did it this time. Next time I speak with Ceto, I need to be here on Earth instead of drifting off into space.*

"Papi, see, I told you I got it."

"Yeah, I see!" I couldn't turn it down now; I didn't want to look like a punk. I grabbed the joint and put it in my pocket like I knew exactly what I was doing. I thought it was a cool reaction. "I'm going to blow this joint down when I get home. I can't wait."

"Nah, fool. That's why we're in the bathroom."

I was nervous, and I had no clue what the hell he'd given me. I knew it was weed because I knew what it smelled like, thanks to having older friends that smoked. I usually just watched—I just never smoked before. I intended to take the joint and throw it in the trash can right before reaching the house. Half of the pressure came from Ceto, and the other half was from me always wanting to try it. Well, here I went, doing my best to avoid smoking, and now the pressure was on.

"I can wait, bro. I don't want to smoke it all at once."

"Papi, come on. You know I got more where that came from. Go ahead, fool. You are acting scared."

Ceto passed me his lighter, and I nervously reached out to grab it. One flick of the lighter and it fell on the floor. I quickly picked it up and tried another flick, and that's when the magic happened. One puff became two, two became three, followed by a strong cough. *Oh man, I'm smoking like a champion.* I looked at Ceto; he was smoking and talking to himself in the mirror. This dude thought he was Scarface. I couldn't front—I was feeling myself even more.

Ceto looked at me, and I looked at him, and we both just started laughing like crazy.

Young Kaz

Right in the middle of us laughing, we heard this loud disruption, the school bell. It scared us to death, and we both jumped and laughed even harder. I guess someone thought they were missing out on the action because they just burst into the restroom. Come to find out, it was Ms. Williams.

My eyes opened wide in amazement, not because I was nervous about getting caught but because she looked more beautiful than ever! She was walking toward me and reaching out to hug me. I watched with a perverted grin as her hand went in the air in slow motion and then came down fast as hell and smacked me on the head. Ms. Williams slapped me so hard, and before I could lift my head up, she began twisting the shit out of my ear. I couldn't laugh anymore because it was hurting. Ceto started laughing at me, but it wasn't long before he was bent over with a twisted ear like mine.

"What the hell is wrong with y'all? Get the hell out of this bathroom and take your ass to class, both of you," was her reply. I wasn't mad at her because she didn't take us to the dean's office. She let us get away but warned us the next time we were going to get in trouble. I looked at Ceto as she let us go, knowing he would say something smart, but there was no reply. He did the same thing I was, rubbing his ear while walking to class. At first, it bothered us, but after we got in the classroom and settled down, the pain went away, and that's when I got the full effect of the weed. Within seconds of looking at the blackboard, I was stoned.

This girl named Vicky came to my table, asking me about something. I can't tell you what she said because I couldn't hear anything—I was stuck and hypnotized watching her lips. *Damn, her lips look smooth and soft*, I thought to myself. "I wonder how they would feel around my bone," I said calmly, speaking to myself. What I failed to realize was I spoke out loud.

"Excuse me, nasty boy!" she replied while blushing. I kept watching her lips. I imagined myself licking her lips at the same time while licking mine. I guess you could say I knew my limits with her now. Thank God she happened to be into me—well, at least, I thought she was.

"I'm sorry, but you have some sexy lips."

"Stop being nasty, you pervert. I only came over to see if you got some more bud."

"Why would you ask me something like that?"

"I know a pothead when I see one. My brother stays high! Anyways, do you?"

Rickey Dudley

I felt like I had the keys to the city the way she came to me, but truthfully, Ceto was the man, not me. I wasn't going to let her know that, of course.

"You already know I got it!"

"Well, you going to give it to me or what?"

"Sure, I'll give you some, but I'm not sure if you can handle it," I said, grabbing my peter bone.

"Stop being nasty, you perv!" Yeah, she caught me out there. I was being sexual with my words, but grabbing my peter bone wasn't in her view, so she had to be following my hand movement. What could I say? I was a player. I had to practice sometimes.

"It's at home, and how is that being a perv? I'm asking if you can handle it. My bud is strong!"

"Yeah, ok then. Yes, I can handle it! I'm not new to this. Bring it tomorrow, punk!" As she left my desk, she pulled her pants up and smirked as the jeans complimented the curves of her butt cheeks, showing me how fat her butt was. While looking at my pelvis area, she replies, "And yes, I can handle that too!"

That was a sexy response, catching me off guard. All I could do was smile at her. Now my mission was getting Ceto to hold me down with extra dud.

I couldn't lie, I was digging this feeling. I just felt relaxed, without stress, and I wasn't even thinking about schoolwork. My thoughts were about Vicky now. I couldn't believe how beautiful she was, and all this time I'd been in class with her, I'd never looked at her in that way until now.

"Hello, Mr. Kaz. Y'all want to tell the class what the big talk was about? We're waiting," said Mr. Bill, the classroom teacher.

"Nothing much. I was just trying to catch up on our work."

"Well, why didn't you just ask me?" he replied.

"Oh, not for this class, Mr. Bill," I said, trying to bring this dialog to an end.

"So, my class is not important?"

For some reason, I was getting a little frustrated now. I felt like he was challenging my manhood while putting me on the spot in front of everyone. *Keep calm, Kaz. Keep calm*, I tell myself.

"Ok, I get it. I should've waited until class was over to get that information."

"Thanks for your honesty, Kaz, but now can you tell the class what it was about? Curious minds want to know. What was the work about from your other class that was so important it caused you to decide to interrupt my classroom?"

Young Kaz

This fucking dude couldn't leave me alone, but for some reason, I started to dig this little challenge.

Ok, Kaz. Come up with something good to make him back him, I said to myself. "We were just talking about the nine stars in the sky that are actually planets."

"Is that right, Ms. Vicky?" Mr. Bill asked. *Come on, say yes*, I said inside, trying to cheer her on.

"Yes, Mr. Bill!"

Good girl, there you go, I thought, feeling proud.

"Ok. Ms. Vicky, how many planets are in the sky?" See, now he was trying to insult our intelligence.

"There are five," she said confidently. "You're wrong, Ms. Vicky, and Kaz, next time, stick to a topic both of y'all know. I'm no fool! Now, where were we, class?"

I felt like a fool—he got that one. Something was out of order; I looked to the back of the class to see Ceto out cold. That explained it. Whenever he was quiet, it was because he was high.

"Ceto, Ceto! Go home and sleep. Don't sleep in my class," Mr. Bill said.

"I'm sorry, Mr. Bill, but I didn't sleep much between your class and my social studies class."

"Young man, I understand. Just try not to sleep in my class, ok? It doesn't look good and is unfair to everyone else."

"Ok, Mr. Bill." Then he had the nerve to look at me and wink his eye as if he just showed me how to get one over on the teacher. That was it? Wasn't the teacher going to challenge him? Why didn't I think of that…

"Ceto, you have your book on you?"

"Yes, sir. I have it right here. I fell asleep reading this chapter in your class, sir."

"Very good"

What?! Ceto was making me look bad. This couldn't be—I was usually the smart one.

"Kaz, turn to chapter eight."

Oh shit, I don't even have my book bag on me. I left it in the locker room. What a way to go, I said to myself, feeling bad.

"Missing something, Kaz?" asked Mr. Bill as he noticed me.

"Yes, I forgot my book. It's in my locker."

"Ok, go and get it."

As I walked past Ceto, he joked at me for slipping, replying, "Yo soy true Papi chulo primo, you heard." We both laughed. I nodded my head, letting him know, *yeah, you got this one*, giving him a pound.

As I made my way to the locker room, I bumped into the janitor lady. I wanted more of what she gave me but didn't know how to ask her for it. Then she spoke, "Hello, Papi. Why are you not in class?"

"I was, but I had forgotten some books near my locker."

"Oh, I'm sorry. I took those to the dean's office."

What the fuck! Damn, now I was really fucked.

Rickey Dudley

I would have to explain why my books were there in the first place. "What did the dean say when you brought the books to him?" I said, sounding worried.

"I'm kidding, Papi. I put them up."

"Where at?"

"Come, Papi. I'll show you because you won't find it if you go without me."

Man, this lady had a fat ass. I was walking behind her, and I didn't know whether she was moving like that on purpose or not, but she had an amazing walk. It looked good from behind. You already know where my mind was going. That urge hit me so bad I walked fast enough to let my hand swing and hit her butt, and suddenly she stopped. "Papi, how was your weekend? Did you enjoy yourself?"

"Yes, I did, thanks, you?"

"Yes, Papi, thanks. I was thinking about you, and I just want to say sorry for that."

"No, it's ok. I liked it. I've been thinking about you ever since that day."

"You want more?" she asked proudly.

"Hell yeah—I mean, yes, please." Yes, just what I wanted! She had me feeling like a kid in a candy store. She started slowly rubbing on my chest, caressing it to get herself in the mood. She went for my lips to kiss me, but I didn't want to kiss her because the thought of her swallowing me made me feel like I was about to kiss my own dick. I had to think quickly because if I didn't give her what she wanted, she wouldn't give me what I wanted. I gave her a little peck on the lips.

"Papi, why you don't kiss me? You don't find me attractive?" I'm sorry if I didn't explain before, but this woman looked like Megan Good in the face, and from behind, she had a butt like Janet Jackson. Man, I loved me some Janet Jackson. She had nice-sized breasts, was about forty, and still looked good. Shit, I would've kissed her before if she hadn't gone down on me and swallowed my sperm.

"No, it's not that. I've just been to the dentist for my tooth, and it still hurts a little bit. I'm trying not to aggravate it," I said.

"Ok, Papi. No worries."

I felt her hands rubbing my peter bone. She began to unzip my pants, pulling me all the way out, and I was just waiting for her to put her lips on it and put me in heaven. Either she was reading my mind, or she couldn't wait to taste me because suddenly, she got down on her knees and went to work.

Young Kaz

Suddenly, we heard a loud noise that came from a walkie-talkie. We both jumped up, looking scared. The sound was getting closer, so I whispered in her ear, "Go to the showers, and I will get them away from here. When I do, you have to sneak out, ok? If you get caught, you have an excuse—just say you decided to clean early." She looked at me and smiled as if we were playing hiding and go seek. I stepped out with my bags and bumped into Ms. Williams.

"Now what the hell are you doing in here? Why aren't you in class, Kaz?"

"I came in here to get my book bag. See?" I showed her.

"Alright, go ahead."

While leaving, I looked back because I was wondering if Ms. Williams was going to go into the locker room to do a check or if she was going to leave. Hopefully the janitor lady didn't get caught.

While I walked back to class, I thought about what could happen if someone found out—I hoped we didn't get in big trouble.

As I entered the classroom, I could see the teacher didn't miss me. But Ceto did. He jumped up, looked at me, and asked, "Where were you?"

I looked at him and laughed, giving him the sign that I was trying to get some head. That was what we called getting our peter bone sucked. I went to my seat, feeling big-headed but unsatisfied because I didn't bust that nut. As soon as I sat in my seat, the bell rang.

While me and Ceto spoke before walking out the classroom door, Vicky tapped me on the shoulder. "Don't forget tomorrow, ok, Kaz." She walked away, smiling.

Ceto gave me this look like he wanted to kill me. "What's up, kid? Why are you looking at me like that?"

"I see you want to be like me, huh?" Then we both laughed, being that he was the supplier.

"I need a favor, kid," I asked without looking desperate.

"See, Papi, I told you."

"Yeah, yeah, you're the true Papi chulo," I said, giving him that satisfaction. "I need more bud, kid."

"For Vicky, right?" he said knowingly. I smiled at him. I didn't want to tell him it was because I wasn't sure if he would hate on me. I took the chance anyway.

"Yeah, boy. What are you so happy about?" I asked.

"You about to smash that? I hit that already. You are getting leftovers, kid." I would hate to admit that I would try and hit, but I always had to stay a step ahead of Ceto; that was just how we did. My plans on getting inside Vicky's pants changed. I wasn't trying to hit anymore.

"She asked me for some bud, so I figured I'd get some from you and give it to her. Did you get head?" I asked, curious to know.

Rickey Dudley

Nah, but I hit. She said she doesn't do things like that, so I just fucked her in the ass."

"What the fuck?"

"What you mean, what the fuck?"

"Nah, bro. That's nasty! You got shit on your dick. How do you expect them to suck it like that?"

"You're right. I didn't think about that. I figured since it's their shit, they can suck it."

"Yeah, you a nasty dog."

"You should try it, bro. That shit feels good and tight too."

"So, you are saying it's better than pussy?"

"Never had pussy. I just like to fuck them in the ass."

"You mean to tell me all this time, when you say you smash, you mean in the ass, not the pussy? Dude!"

"Hell yeah. That shit is funny. I had one girl jump up like, hold on, I got to dodo!"

This conversation was nasty as hell, but his face while telling me these stories made me roll in tears. "Papi, please wait, and when I pulled out, she jumped up and ran to the restroom."

"I'm going to call you a shithead from now on," I told him.

"Yeah, ok. You going to have that name soon, you'll see. Ms. Rodriguez is going to get that ass, you watch."

"Ms. Rodriguez? Who the fuck is that—a Spanish voodoo lady spirit or some shit?" I asked, thinking that he was putting a spell on me.

"Oh, you didn't find out yet. I can't wait until you do. I'm going to laugh my ass off." He got to me there, but I had to shake it off. He was always playing around or lying about something.

"As far as the bud, I'll bring it to you tomorrow, or you can come to my house and get it."

"Yeah, bring it tomorrow," I told him. I was going to go to his house and get it, but I was as high as a kite. I would rather go home and sleep this shit off before my mom caught me.

"Yo, add a little bit on the side for me," I said.

"Tell you what, I'll give you an ounce. That's off the arm from me, but after that, you have to buy!" Ceto said, sounding like a businessman.

"Fair game. Good looking out, bro."

While heading home, my mind was rumbling with thoughts. I guessed it was the weed because normally my mind was clear. I was enjoying this feeling but also wondering what my mom's reaction would be if she saw me high. *Ok, here we go.* I walked into the house, and all I heard was laughter and Mom and Malvin having a good time. I stopped in amazement because I hadn't seen Mom laugh like that in a long time unless she was talking with me or my aunties.

"Hey, baby. How was school?"

Young Kaz

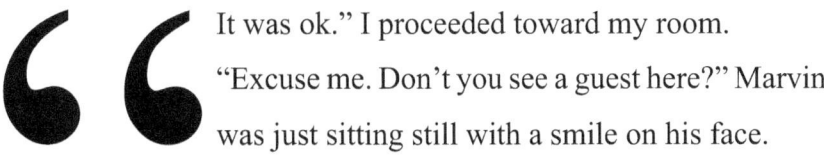It was ok." I proceeded toward my room. "Excuse me. Don't you see a guest here?" Marvin was just sitting still with a smile on his face.

"What's up, dude!"

"Excuse me. He has a name."

"Nah, it's cool, no worries. I'm alright with that," Marvin said.

"That's fine with you, but I'm not. I'm waiting, mister."

"Hey, Marvin."

"Thank you, baby!"

I guess I was being a little stubborn, but I wasn't ready to accept him yet. Mom was, and from the looks of it, he was not going anywhere anytime soon.

I headed to my bedroom, free at last. What was this? A phone in my room? I turned around, and Mom was standing there with Marvin at the door, which was now open. "Come on, Ma. You are invading my privacy."

"Ok, baby, but I wanted to see your expression."

"Thanks, but how much do I have to pitch in?"

"Well, you have to ask Marvin that. It was his idea." I could see he was trying to win me over for my mom, and I wasn't ready to let him take my pop's place, so I just kind of nodded to him while replying, "Ok, Marvin, how much do I have to pitch in?"

"It's already paid for. I got the bill. Just do me a favor and be responsible, and don't go crazy with it."

"Fair game," I said.

"Oh, shoot. I got the food on the stove. Excuse me, y'all."

"Hey, champ, can I rap with you for a moment?"

"Ok, so that's how I'm paying for it, by letting you talk to me?" I responded.

"Nah, it's not like that, I just—" Right before he could say anything else, I just wrote him off by turning my back on him.

"Alright, then. I'd rather you not speak right now.

"Ok, champ! That's the type of time you're on. Cool."

He walks away in disappointment. Before I could say anything else, I noticed his back was turned with the door closing. I may have been too hard on him, but he would get over it.

I lay on my back, looking up at the ceiling, over-excited about my phone. I picked it up and dialed any number that came to mind. When someone answered and asked who it was, I'd reply, "Who is this? You called my phone," and then hang up, laughing my butt off.

I was still high, so I did that for about twenty minutes, then decided to sleep. Suddenly, this noise woke me up, and it was the phone ringing. I did find it kind of cool to have my own phone now.

"Hello?"

"The food is done. You want me to make your plate now?"

"It's ok. I'm not hungry now."

"Ok."

Rickey Dudley

As I reached over to hang up the phone, I realized there was a little note, and it read:

Dear Kaz,

I got this phone for you, hoping you would like it, and no, I'm not trying to win you over for your mom. I have her already. My life is not complete until you are in it. I have strong feelings for your mother, and when a man accepts a woman, he accepts everything that comes with that woman. I want to get to know you because I plan on being in your life as well, so whenever you need me, my number is installed on the phone. Press and hold the number two button, and it will automatically call me, and press and hold the number one for the same with your mom. P.s., Turn the phone over, and you will find your number on the back of it. Take care, champ. Also, no one can replace your pops! He was the best!

Shit, after reading this, I felt really bad about how I treated Marvin. Back to bed, I went.

Time had passed, and the phone rang again. D.M.X's song "Ain't No Way" blasted out. I loved that song. I reached to answer the phone, and the music was still playing. Oh shit, it was an alarm. It was already school time, so I jumped up to get ready for school, doing my daily hygiene norm, and I could smell Mom cooking breakfast.

"Hey, good morning, Ma."

"Good morning, baby. I see you're up just in time."

"I thought the phone was ringing, but it was the alarm. You got me on that one. That was nice, Ma. How did you set the alarm like that, though?"

"Oh, baby. You'd have to ask Marvin about that. He said you would like it!"

Yeah, I feel stupid now, I thought.

"By the way, take that money off the table by the T.V."

"Ok, hold up, Ma. It's fifty dollars here?"

"I know. Can I get twenty-five out of that?"

I looked at my mom's face, and I already knew the answer to my question before I even asked. "Marvin, right?"

"Yes, baby. He's really a good role model for you. You know I wouldn't bring anyone around you if they weren't right. You need a man in your life, baby. There are just some things I can't do as a woman that a man can do for you, and that's to teach you how to be a man, a responsible man with good judgment. Don't forget to wash your plate out before you leave for school, okay? Love you. Have a good day."

Damn, Mom was kicking out that knowledge early this morning. As I walked out, I thought about everything, even Marvin this time. Maybe I should give him a chance.

While walking to school, my plans changed for the day. My mission was to just get that bud from Ceto and give some to Vicky—maybe get a little head if possible.

While walking into school, Ms. Williams gave me this look that was just a little different from before.

Young Kaz

"Good morning, Ms. Williams," I replied with a smile. Her reply was different.

"Good morning, June-bug." Now I knew the story behind June-bug, but damn, she knew my name. Why would she call me June-bug?

"Ms. Williams, my name is—"

Right before I could finish, she replied in a nasty tone that I never heard her in before, "I know what the hell your name is. Get the hell out of my face and get to class!"

Ok, that just messed up all the chakras in my body and fucked my head up.

"Kaz!" Ceto yelled. I looked at Ceto and then looked back at Ms. Williams. I noticed she wasn't herself; she seemed down and out.

"Ceto, go ahead, man. I'll catch up with you later," I yelled back.

"You forgot?"

"Nah, it's going to be quick. I just want to speak with Ms. Williams real quick."

"Alright, I'll be in the gym."

I may have been playing myself, but Ms. Williams' attitude bothered me. Maybe I should just leave her alone, but something inside me just wouldn't let it go. I had to know what was going on. Even though I like her, I always gave Ms. Williams the utmost respect.

"Ms. Williams?" She just stared at me. "I thought I was your favorite. Why are you talking to me in a nasty tone? I didn't do anything to you."

"No, you didn't, Kaz, and I'm sorry, but I was hurt when I saw you smoking and ditching class in the bathroom. We just talked about June-bug and how he messed himself up in life, and you are heading down the same road. I was disappointed in you," she said with brutal honesty.

"Well, don't be. I'm still on point. I'm doing good in all my classes, and thanks for caring about me."

"No problem, little guy. Bring it in." As she reached out to me indicating a hug—*yes, my hormones are running wild, and the phrase is true; young, dumb, and full of come*—the only thing I could think of was the feeling of being close to her, and man, I couldn't describe it. I just knew she smelled amazing.

I wondered if she smelled like that in the morning. Her breasts were pressed against my chest. *Oh no, not now.* My peter bone began to rise. I backed out just a little, sticking my butt out, but to her, it must have felt like I didn't want to hug her. While laughing, she pulls me in tighter and gets a hell of a surprise.

"Boy!" she replied in shock as she bounced back from feeling the poke in my pants.

"I'm sorry. I'm very sensitive. Got to go now." I smirked just a little as I ran off to class.

"Yeah, ok, take your little nasty butt on!" She smiled at me in disbelief. Well, at least she knew it wasn't on purpose.

Rickey Dudley

I I almost forgot about Vicky, so I first had to check Ceto for that bud. Knowing exactly where he would be, I headed straight to the gym.

"Ceto!" I yelled, grabbing his attention.

"Copy, bro. Hold on."

While standing on the sideline, I saw Vicky laughing with her friends. Now that I thought of it, she was not bad looking after all. This time she had on black pants that fit her nicely. There was something about a girl with a body in black that drove me crazy.

"Hey, Kaz!"

"Yo, what are you doing in the gym with no gym clothes on?"

"Same reason you in here without yours!"

"I'm the new mascot," I told her, being funny.

"Yeah, right. Stop playing before I punch you." I flexed as she went in for a light blow, and shit, she made me want to fight her from how hard she hit.

"I'll have that smoke for you soon. I'll bring it to class later."

"Nah, why can't I come and get it from you?"

"Well, I live up the block if you want to stop by my house later."

"Sure, that's cool. How much do I have to bring?"

"Nothing, it's cool. It's on me." Now I'd put my foot in my own ass. Why in the hell did I invite her to my house? My mom would kill me. Shit, and on top of that, I had to carry the smoke the whole day until class ended. *Yeah, way to go, Kaz.*

"Okay, see you later." As she walked away, I was really thinking about tapping that ass. She had this walk on her like she knew she was the shit, but what I liked most about her was that she was down to earth. She knew she was sexy but didn't let it go to her head. On top of that, she had a nice sense of humor, and her attitude reminded me of my mom—just cool as fuck.

"Oh yeah, Papi. What's up? I put that on top of your locker."

"Okay, now you want to tell me what possessed you to do that? You could get me in trouble like that, man."

"Stop bitching. No one is going to fuck with your locker. Besides, I'd rather it be on top of the locker instead of being on you."

"You're right. I didn't think about that. On second thought, how the hell do you know where my locker is? I changed it."

"Bro!" he said.

"Yeah, you are the Papi chulo." We both laughed.

Ever since I'd met Ceto, he'd been good to me, like a brother from another mother.

I was on my way to class thinking about what Ms. Williams said about June-bug. It made me want to work harder in school, so I made up my mind and had a good talk with Ceto.

Young Kaz

I was amazed; he was following my lead. I clearly told him, "Look, you're my brother, you know that, but now I need to focus on school and bang these grades out, bro. So from now on, we've got to tighten up and only have fun after school, not during class." and he replied, "I'm with you, bro."

While we were sitting in class, doing our work, I could feel eyes on me. It was like they were burning a hole through my head. I went to look up and saw Vicky watching me with her pencil in her mouth. Shit, in my mind, I thought, *Damn, that shit is sexy*, but I still maintained my cool.

"Why are you looking at me like that?"

She replied, "Oh, please, no one is looking at you. I'm daydreaming."

"Yeah, ok. Just don't choke on that pencil, or your ass will be daydreaming from the hospital." Suddenly my chair jolted from a kick from Ceto.

"Bro, fun after class, remember!"

"Yeah, you're right, bro. Thanks!"

Back to the books, my mind went from one class to the next. Now I found myself puzzled—why was it that every history class just spoke about Dr. Martin Luther King and Malcolm X? Now I didn't have a problem with either, but I was sure other famous people had high achievements, like Elijah Muhammad, Fred Hampton, and Colon Powers. Who became the highest chief in the military? But I guess that was how it was—to keep black people at a low frequency.

When I woke up out of my daydream, the bell rang. Today went kind of fast, just how I liked it. As I was leaving, Ceto reminded me that the bud was on top of my locker. "Don't forget to get that, bro. If you do sell it, remember nickel bags are five dollars, and dime bags are ten dollars. I gave you just a little more bagged already, so you don't have to worry about anything. That's all I put in, anyway. Just nickels and dimes."

"Good looking, bro!"

"Excuse me, Ceto. Can I speak with you for a second, Kaz?"

"I'll catch you later, bro."

"Bet. Vicky, what's up?"

"I can't make it over right now. Is it ok if I swing by later? I'll have the money then."

"That's cool. You can just pick it up later. Even though I told you I got you, if you want to pay, that's cool."

"Nah, I like to support. I'll bring the money. I just wanted to make sure that coming by a little later was cool. If anything, here's my number. Just call me any time after seven."

"Alright, cool," I said.

While I walked out of the school, I thought, *What the hell did I just do? I had the smoke on me. I could've given it to her then,* but the thought of her coming over to my house—yeah, that part— was the reason I withheld. But did I really play myself? First of all, my mother was going to be home around that time, and how the hell was I going to call her? *Yeah, I fucked up this time.*

Rickey Dudley

I t dawned on me that I had the phone in my room, thanks to Marvin, but how was I going to get my mom out of the house? *Marvin!* Thinking about just gave me an idea. With him in the way, my mom might go a little easy on me. Maybe I could get him to take her out.

While I raced to the house, I began to slow down when thinking about my encounter with him last night, so plan A was out the window, and plan B was gone too. Plan A was calling Vicky, and plan B was convincing Marvin to take my mom out. By the time I got home, I was exhausted. Suddenly, the phone rang in my room, and I lit up again, knowing I still had the phone.

"Hello?"

"Hey, baby. I'm going to be home a little late today, ok? But I've asked Marvin to stop by and check on you."

"Ok."

After seeing how Marvin could be a great resource to me, I realized it wasn't so bad after all having him around. After hanging up the phone, I looked around my room for anything out of place, but everything was good. My mom always made sure I kept the habit of keeping my room clean—I loved her for that. Not to brag, but my room was laced up; hip hop section and library section—shit, I even had a movie section. There was no reason for me to ever leave my room except to eat dinner.

I couldn't lie, it wasn't the thirst for Vicky that made me call. I guess it was me having my own phone and using it for the first time that got me open. I started dialing Vicky's number, and right when I was about to hang up, I heard a man's voice.

"Yo, who is this?"

"It's Kaz. Can I please speak with Vicky?"

"Vicky don't live here, nigga."

In the background, I heard her voice, and suddenly the phone hung up. I was confused and in disbelief. I just hung the phone up on my end, as I did get a little scared. Then the phone rang back.

"Hello?"

"Hey, you just called. It's Vicky."

"Yes, it's me, Kaz."

"Oh, what's up, K.K.?"

I was a little lost, but K.K. seemed pretty cool for a nickname. While she spoke, I could hear in the background, "Hurry up off the phone. I'm waiting for a phone call."

"Ma! Tell Mickey to leave me alone!"

"Sorry, K.K., my brother is acting like an ass."

"It's cool." I chuckle and listen to her sweet voice.

"I told you to call me about seven, fool."

"Yeah, I thought about it after I dialed your number, but it was too late."

"Yeah, I know, sometimes I do shit on impulse when I'm high!" she laughed. I couldn't tell her the truth, so I went along as if the weed made me forget.

"Listen, I'll call you back after seven now that I have your number, ok?" said Vicky.

"No problem. I have nothing but time on my hands now."

Suddenly the doorbell rang. *Who the fuck is this now?*

Young Kaz

As I walked to the door, I yelled, "Who is it?"

"Marvin!" he yelled back. Wow, now that caught me off guard. I knew he was supposed to check on me, but damn, he could've called.

"Hey, what's up, Marvin?"

"Hey, what's up, champ? Your mom asked me to check on you."

"Yeah, she told me you were going to stop by. Come in. First of all, I just want to apologize for my actions the other day. I was just tired."

"It's cool. I understand."

"I got the letter that you wrote and the fifty dollars you left for me. For starters, you don't have to do all these things for me. I see how happy my mom is with you, and I accept you being in her life. Just treat her right."

"That means a lot. Thanks! For the record, the money was just coming from my heart. I always love hard. As for you, once again, I'm not your father. I could never replace him—his shoes are too big for me, but I'll tell you what I can do: my best to raise you and help you to grow as a man. You don't have to call me Dad. Marvin is fine by me. All I ask is that you give me a chance and show respect," he said, sounding sincere.

"Sound good. I'll think about it… Lol, I'm kidding. I agree."

"Cool, I see someone is using the phone."

"Yeah, it's coming in handy."

"I bet. You going to let the phone ring all day?" he said with a jester, indicating that it was ringing. "Huh? Oh shit. Vicky!"

I rushed to my room, hoping I caught it, almost out of breath. "Hello?"

"Can I come over now? I'm free."

"Sure you can. You know how to get here, right?"

"Silly, didn't you say you live a block or so from the school?"

"Yeah."

"Well I'm not too far, either. I'm about four blocks away, so I'll be there soon."

"Ok, it's the red house on your left as you come down the block at the back of the school."

"Ok." Immediately, I hung up the phone and rushed back into the living room where Marvin was. "Marvin, I need a big favor, man."

"What's up?"

"See, I got this girl coming over, but I told her I was home alone. I don't know what time my mom is coming home today. I was hoping you would pick her up and take her out, and by doing that, I could spend a little time with her. It's all innocent."

"Now if I get in trouble, I'm bringing you down with me." Yeah, this dude was not bad after all. I think this was where our relationship could start. "By the way, make sure you strap up, and Kaz, next time you decide to smoke, make sure you put some cologne on and be responsible. Don't smoke when you are in school, and most definitely don't just smoke in the streets."

Rickey Dudley

What the hell? How did he know I was smoking? "You're right. Did Mom notice?" I asked. "Nah, she didn't notice it. At first, I thought it was outside, but when I looked at you, that's when I knew." We both laughed, acknowledging I was stoned.

"So, that's why you were stuck there smiling the other day." I couldn't lie, this guy was really cool. My mom said I would like having him around. If we were vibing now, I could only imagine what it would be like hanging out with him.

"Hell yeah. I remember the first time I smoked—"

Right before we could get into the conversation, there were three hard knocks at the door. "Open up. It's the police!"

Me and Marvin looked at each other in disbelief.

"Don't look at me. I'm not opening that door," Marvin whispered to me. Don't ask me why Marvin and I acted like we had just committed a major crime, both scared to open the door. We sat quietly, hoping the police would go away, but who were we fooling? Shit, even I knew after a while they were just going to kick the door in. Maybe someone gave me up, telling the cops I got weed. Holy shit, I did have weed in my room. Truthfully, I would rather open the door than let them break it down because if my mom came home and saw that shit, me, the cops, and Marvin were in trouble.

I slowly walked toward the door, but then it dawned on me. "Say, Marvin, on second thoughts, you're the man of the house. Why don't you open the door?" I whispered to him, laughing and moving far away back toward my room.

It caught me off guard a little because Marvin started talking louder, saying, "Kaz, open the door for the cops, man." I paused and gave him that Kevin Hart serious stare, wondering why he'd dime me out like that.

He began laughing and walking to open the door. I heard, "Oh, I'm sorry, mister." Damn, it was Vicky. She scared the hell out of me.

"Kaz," Marvin replied while still laughing at me. "I'm heading out now. I'll call you later." Marvin started walking out the door, and Vicky began walking in, and I noticed he gave me the ok sign, symbolizing that Vicky looked good.

Vicky had these white pants on, and you could see her black panty line, black and white Jordans with a nice white T-shirt that was hanging slightly, just enough to show one of her shoulders with black letters that read on the front "*yes I am*" and on the back "*sexy & I know it*" and smelling like sweet candy. I was amazed, like it was my first time seeing her. Her hair was straight. She had a pretty smile and no makeup on. For some reason, she just looked sexy as hell.

"So, what up, big head?"

"What's up? You look cute," I told her.

"Shit, cute doesn't describe me. I'm a bad chick." We both laughed as she did a Lil Kim move.

Young Kaz

This weird thought came to mind of her being my girlfriend, but I knew that was out the window because Ceto said he had slept with her already. "Wait right here. Let me get the bud."

"Yeah, you're right. I don't want to see your dirty ass room. I know how dirty you guys can be."

"On second thought, why don't you come in? I want to show you something." That was just my way of luring her into my bedroom, so she could see that she was wrong—my mama didn't raise no slob.

"Boy, please. You won't be bragging to your friends, letting them know you had me in your room. Sorry, I'm not that type of girl." I wanted to believe her, but knowing Ceto slept with her, I knew she had an idea that I knew too.

Luring her in my room, yeah, she was right about that, but I just wanted her to see that my room was clean. "Oh, ok, so I see you're a revolution type of brother, huh? Nice. Hard to come by, but nice," she replied, impressed.

"Look at you. I never thought I would hear that come out of your mouth."

"Why is that?"

"Well, in school, you don't strike me as the knowledge type, you know? Like, into your work."

"I am. I just don't find their teaching entertaining."

"Fine, but can I ask you what the hell a water planet is?"

We both stared at each other for a second and burst into tears laughing.

"Yeah, I know, right? I was high."

She admired my room, checking out all my posters and pictures. She stopped by Assata Shakur and Sara Baartman, looking on in amazement but curiosity. Suddenly, she paused and then turned her head toward me, on the same side her naked shoulder was on, and said, "Ok, I was about to give you even more respect for Assata Shakur, but this here, yeah—you are a freak! An older lady, naked? What is wrong with you?"

"See, now a woman of your class should understand this picture." I walked up behind her and reached over her to fix the picture she tilted. "This is not an ordinary picture. Her name is Ms. Sara Baartman. She was the first video vixen.

"Back in her time, she was a slave. Her oppressor used to have her stand up in front of everybody, naked, while some poked her body in amazement. They'd never really seen a woman with such a beautiful body. Anyway, she went through some tough times. If you do your research on her, you will understand why wear tight clothes today."

"Wow, that's crazy. I think I will do a little research, but do you think me wearing tight clothes is bad?"

"Oh no, you look beautiful. I'm a man at the end of the day, but I do love a woman who respects her body."

Rickey Dudley

"" I really like your mentality. There are not too many guys out here that think like you." She walked toward me, close enough to kiss me but stopped just enough for me to have breathing space. We stared into each other's eyes for a second or two.

I felt like it was the right time; my body suddenly started setting fireworks off inside, and this uncontrollable feeling came over me. I don't know what it was, but it led me to dive in for a kiss. Then she snatched the bud out of my hand and smiled.

"Look at you, nasty, trying to kiss me." She smiled while speaking.

"No, I wasn't."

I reached out for the exchange, waiting for her to put the money in my hand. She attempted to put the money in my hand, but before I knew it, the money went back into her pocket, so I did what anybody would do. I went reaching to take the money out of her pocket. I think it was a good move because we went from tussling to wrestling on the bed, and then there we were, face to face, me on top of her with her hands pinned down and nowhere for her to run. Our hearts were racing, and we were both gasping for air. I was staring at her, and you could see a little sweat forming on her baby hair. Her eyes were putting me in a trance, and I could feel her heart beating through my palms; it was all or nothing at this point.

I went for that kiss again, and she did not stop me this time. We kissed so passionately, and it was something new to me. I had never experienced this before, but I knew it all just felt too good. Knowing I had her right where I wanted her, I reached toward her breast and began to caress one of them. She grabbed my hand and stopped me.

"I'm sorry. I can't do this," Vicky replied.

"Nah, it's ok. I'm not going to tell Ceto." I thought by me saying that she would just keep going along with it, but that pissed her off. Within seconds, she was going green like the she-hulk. She got strength from the Gods and threw me off of her onto the floor.

"What the fuck does that mean?" I was speechless and didn't know how to come back from that one. "Never mind. I already know word has been around school that Ceto smashed! All of you guys are the same. Just when I thought that maybe you would be different!"

Now I was really feeling confused by the reaction, aside from me messing the mood up. I found myself thinking that maybe Ceto didn't smash. That look she gave me while trying to reclaim her innocence felt sincere.

That's when it happened, a voice I wasn't ready to hear. Mom. "Kaz, you here?" and then the phone rang. Now I was fucked because Vicky wasn't supposed to be here, and if I picked the phone up, she would know I was here and might want to come in the room.

Young Kaz

This might have been Vicky's lucky day, her seeing me get my ass beat. I yelled, "Yeah, Ma. Hold on!" as I reached for the phone, signaling Vicky not to say anything.

"Hello?"

"Did your mom get there?"

"Yeah, thanks for the heads up," I said, disappointed.

"Nah, you good. I told her you were studying. She's coming in, but she's heading right back out. I'm out front waiting on her. I'm taking her to the movies."

"Alright, cool, thanks." I rushed out, leaving Vicky in the room, hoping my mom didn't get to my door before I did.

"Mom, what happened?" I said, trying to sound innocent.

"Nothing, baby. Just wanted to let you know Marvin is taking me to the movies, ok? You need anything?"

"Nope, I'm ok."

"Ok, well if you do go back out, make sure you're in at eleven thirty, ok? It's nine now. I should be back around one or two o'clock."

After getting through that close call, I rushed back to my room to check on Vicky. "Sorry about that."

"Is the coast clear now?"

"Yes," was my reply with a smile, but I noticed she wasn't smiling. She got up and walked out, going toward the door, but right before opening the door to leave, she turned around with that beautiful naked shoulder and replied, "Thanks for the weed. I left the money near your picture, and for the record, Ceto didn't smash, and neither did you!"

Damn, I felt fucked up inside, but I really thought he smashed. I saw him hugging her that day, but then again, he hugged all the girls like that, and they were cool back in the day.

The night was young, and now I was home alone. I went toward my room to retrieve the money. It was funny because all I could think about was that moment we paused right before we kissed. I was going crazy now. I glanced at the pictures to see which one she put the money near, and then I spotted it on the Sara Baartman picture. I just paused and looked at it. I didn't even bother to check how much she put there. I just left it there as a reminder of Vicky. There was so much I could do in my room, but at this moment, I just wanted to lay back and reflect on what went down between her and I.

I lay on my bed, and I could still smell her sweet candy perfume. The only way I could stop this feeling was by going to sleep. And the only way to do that was to roll a nice joint; the potency from the weed smelled so strong. I knew how to roll because, like I said, I had always been around professionals. I did well for my first. It wasn't tight like how Ceto did his joints, but it was good enough. I puffed until it was gone. You could now say I was an official pothead.

Rickey Dudley

After smoking the whole joint and daydreaming for a few, I fell sound asleep. Time seemed short because it wasn't long before I heard my alarm going off. I jumped up right away, knowing it was already time for school. I glanced at the picture of Ms. Sara Baartman and the money in the frame, which reminded me of Vicky. By the time I had gotten out of the shower, Mom had breakfast ready for me. I sat down to enjoy my breakfast, and I could feel Mom's eyes on me.

"So, you're going to act like you don't see me watching you, huh?" she replied with a funny face.

"Mom, come on, I'm eating!" I laughed while almost spilling the food out my mouth.

"I spoke with Marvin yesterday."

"About?"

"Well, that depends on which topic you want to talk about first. Better yet, how about after school, we finish this conversation? I'm looking forward to it. I really want to see how you respond to this one."

Right before I could ask what she was talking about, she kissed me on the forehead and went out the door, her last words leaving me in a frenzy. "Think about it because how you respond to it might lead to an ass whooping or punishment. Love you."

The door closed, and my mouth hung open, not knowing what to do.

Finishing my breakfast helped me to calm down. On my way to school, the day felt different than others. I knew it was going to be drama when I got home—*shit, my mom may unalive me*. I'm thinking to myself, *Did Marvin tell her about Vicky being in the room? Oh shit! Even worse, he probably told her about the weed. Wow, I'm a dead man walking*. The next thing I noticed was my senses starting to heighten. I could hear the birds singing their beautiful melodies and squirrels racing in the trees before seeing them.

I stopped at the corner, and I heard that grumpy old voice. "That's it, son. Take your time and pay attention to life." When I focused on the voice, I realized it was the grumpy old man that always seemed to yell at me when I crossed the street. He was standing beside me, waiting for the light as well.

"You're right, sir. Enjoy your day," I said to him and proceeded to school. I thought to myself, *What is life about?* Shit, all I knew was being responsible for your actions and knowing the difference between right and wrong, thanks to Mom. I guessed that other stuff came as you got older. It seemed like the threat of a butt-whooping from your mom or dad always made a kid wise up.

"Good morning, young man. Make today a good day now. Knowledge is power," said Ms. Williams.

"Good morning, Ms. Williams. I see you're perky this morning."

"Yup, just glad to live another day," she said with pride.

"Ok, see you."

"Yo, Kaz, what's up, bro? How was that bud?"

"Man, that bud was good, bro. That shit put me to sleep," I told him.

"Now you see why I fall asleep in class. You feel so relaxed and stress-free, you know."

"Word," I said.

Here we went again, homeroom, then gym class. I was in the mood for a good game of basketball. It had been a while since I played, and you know I was going to come back like Michael Jordan in the last quarter. Although I was doing my thing, I got so distracted when I smelled that sweet scent that helped me sleep. Not the weed; it was Vicky's scent.

But it wasn't Vicky. Some girl was wearing the same perfume. Before I knew it, I was out of bounds.

"Come on, bro. You still in the game or what?" Ceto shouted.

"Yeah, my bad, bro. I felt lightheaded for a minute." The game was on, and we played until the bell rang. Although we were leading, we were still playing hard, trying to wipe them out with a low score. Once the bell rang, we collected everything and headed to the locker room to freshen up and prepare for our next class. We all were talking shit to each other while walking the halls, and then a shout came from the exit door. "Y'all, quiet down. People are still in class, you know!"

We all stopped talking and just looked at Ms. Williams and laughed; we were really having a good time enjoying each other's company. Then the conversation started—you know, the scorecard. For those that don't know, the scorecard is the number of girls you've had sex with. One of the guys brought up some girls' names in the school I was surprised that they had sex with. Still, I hadn't heard Vicky's name. It was Ceto's turn, and I was just waiting to hear Vicky's name. "Word. Monica, Jessica, Israel, and Rodriguez," he said.

Hold on, why haven't I heard Vicky? This must be a mistake, so I helped him out. "Oh, and don't forget Vicky," I insisted.

Two dudes looked at me as if I was just cracking the code to Pandora's box. "Nah, hell no. Ceto didn't beat. I tried, and my game is better than his. I know for a fact he didn't smash. I've known her since junior high school. All I got was a kiss on the cheek," said one guy.

"Well at least you got that. Shit, I didn't get no play at all/ She's one of those good girls, waiting for Mr. Right," said the other guy.

104

"When was this?" I asked curiously as if I were investigating them.

"At the beginning of this school year, but I didn't get the draws. I just got that damn kiss on the cheek."

"Oh yes, she kissed me on the cheek and said I wasn't her type." That's when I was put on the spot by Ceto. I would have been proud to admit I smashed, but I just couldn't lie.

"Well, so what I didn't smash?" Ceto replied. I gave Ceto this look as if I'd just found out his true colors. He disappointed me, and at the same time, I thought back to Vicky's facial expression with her response, *"CETO DIDN'T SMASH!"*

"But my boy Kaz beat it yesterday," Ceto said.

"Nah, I didn't smash," I responded.

"I thought you said that she was coming to your house?" Ceto replied, looking confused.

"Nah, she didn't. I met her by the school, and we just talked," I replied, shutting him down.

We got off that topic, and guys one and two went to their lockers. Ceto's locker was next to mine, but I just looked at him and smiled in disgrace.

"What, bro?"

"Why'd you lie? I thought you really beat."

"So what, bro? I beat it in my dreams. That still counts to me." We both laughed it off.

"Yeah, something is really wrong with your brain, bro."

Everyone else went to their class except me. I was puzzled and literally trying to kick myself in the ass, realizing that I'd gotten the furthest with Vicky than anyone. That's when I heard the sound of the broom and dustpan. What do you know? The janitor lady was coming around cleaning. She knocked on the locker room door. "Is anyone in here?"

I didn't respond. I just waited for her to come in. There was something about knowing a girl likes you and you can experiment. I knew what she liked already, so I did whatever came to my mind. First, I thought about standing on the bench naked again—*no, that's old.* I pulled my pants off and stepped into the shower area. When she came inside, I whispered, "Mommy, come?"

"No, Papi! I can't."

"Please, Mommy? I've been waiting for you. I missed you," I pleaded, yarning for her touch.

I continued, and it was just a matter of time before she gave in. I saw how she was looking down at my peter bone, smiling while saying, "No, Papi."

I grabbed my peter bone and pointed it toward her, saying, "See, Mommy? He misses you! No one takes care of him like you do." At this point, she was getting closer and looking around just to make sure the coast was clear. She started to caress my peter bone.

I don't know what overcame me because I grabbed her and pulled her close, like a pit bull taking back what was his.

"Oh, Papi. I see you did miss me." I had pulled her so close to me I could smell her breathing. We paused just a little bit, and then it happened. She reached in to kiss me.

At that point, I didn't care to think about her swallowing my sperm, so we kissed passionately. I began exploring her body with my hands in a slow fashion. Before I knew it, her pants were down. I couldn't believe it; I was shocked because I'd had sex, but that was only in my dreams. That's when it happened. I felt her grabbing my peter bone as she bent over. She stroked it one last time before inserting it inside her.

Young Kaz

I felt the tightness, but when I looked down, I noticed she was putting my peter bone in her butt. I said to myself, *No, stop her before it goes in. You're going to have shit on your peter bone.* But at the same time, it felt so good, so I just exhaled and went with the flow.

"Papi, pump slow, ok?" she cried softly.

"Ok, Mommy." I began pumping as slowly as I could.

"Ok, Papi, now a little faster so you can come quick." I pumped like she said, but at the same time, I thought about where I was going to drop my load. It was like she read my mind with her response.

"Papi, don't worry. Just come inside me." I pumped a little harder, putting it all inside her. She replied, "Ouch, Papi. Too hard!" I went back to pumping, and that's when I felt that tingling feeling like a lightning bolt through my body, and out came the sperm.

"Papi, you feel good now?" she replied, pulling up her pants.

"Yes, I feel wonderful!" I made sure I washed my peter bone before rushing to my math class. Right before I could touch the doorknob, the bell rang. Class was ending, so that meant science class was next.

As I walked into class, I saw Ceto. "We got to talk, kid," I told him. "Copy, bro. After class, remember?"

"Yeah, my bad. Sure," I replied with a smile.

I looked back and forth between the teacher and Ceto. I was so excited to tell him I just fucked the janitor lady in the ass. I couldn't wait, so I leaned in and said. "Yo! I beat it, kid."

To my surprise, I heard a rude voice. "Move so I can get by!" It was Vicky. My mouth dropped, hoping she didn't hear me and think I was talking about her.

"Yeah, boy. I knew you were going to do it, kid. Was that ass sweet or what?" he replied as Vicky walked by. I cut our conversation short and tried to get Vicky's attention, but she wasn't having it.

I went to grab her hand, and she screamed at me, "Get the fuck off my hand," out loud. It was loud enough to catch the teacher's attention.

"What's going on back there?" Mr. Armstrong yelled.

Oh no, not this, I said to myself. This little outburst may get heated. It reminded me of getting in trouble with Mom. Speaking of trouble, I'm already on bad terms with Mom. I don't need more trouble on top of that.

"Vicky, are you ok?"

"Yes, sir. Sorry for the outburst." She sat down, looking sad, and all I could think about was she probably thought I was talking about her. I was doing my best to let her know it wasn't. I couldn't even get a look from her—it was like she was disgusted with me.

"What's up, bro? Talk to me. Forget her," Ceto said.

Rickey Dudley

If she was close enough to hear our conversation, maybe it would be good to explain to Ceto and give a false story and a fake girl's name. I figured if Vicky heard it, she would see I wasn't talking about her.

"Yeah, man. Shorty was fine. I met her at my mom's job." As I was talking, I could see Vicky leaning back just a little bit to ear hustle. "I think she's mixed Chinese and Jamaican."

"What, bro?" Ceto asked. My plan was working with Vicky, but I was confusing the shit out of Ceto. I had to find a way to cut the conversation short with Ceto.

Suddenly, Vicky interrupted, "Excuse me, Mr. Armstrong, can you tell Kaz to keep his big mouth shut? I'm trying to listen to what you're saying."

I guess in her case, she felt like she was doing something big, but really, she was helping me out because I didn't want to spill all the beans in class anyway.

"Excuse me, Kaz. If you want to talk, get up and go out of my classroom," Mr. Armstrong said.

"Sorry, Mr. Armstrong. I'm done." I gave her this look as if she had accomplished her goal of distracting our conversation by telling. I could smell that sweet perfume she had on, and man, it was driving me crazy. I thought about the kiss we had and wondered what was on her mind. While class went on, every now and then, I would glance over to look at her and see if she was watching me, but no luck at all. I guess she was really upset with me. Doing what I do best, I really zoned out this time because the moment I woke up from daydreaming, the bell rang. I wanted to move, but something inside me just wouldn't let me. I waited for Vicky to get up first.

I just had to see her face. *Come on. Crack a smile or something, girl. Show me we're good*, I told myself in desperation. Suddenly, she got up, and it was like everything went in slow motion. First, her hair as she flung it over her shoulder to get it out her face, then her body as she turned toward me. I had to position myself so that when she got up and turned, she would walk right into me, and what could I say? Perfect timing.

"Excuse me. You're in my way," she said. I really wanted to speak, but I couldn't. I paused and watched her as she spoke, but I just heard quietness while watching her lips move.

"Go ahead. Kiss her already!" Ceto shouted. I could always count on him to mess things up. I decided to let her go by without any further interruption. When she passed, I felt a slight bump, and when she went by me, she left a nice scent of her perfume in the air. I closed my eyes just for a second to enjoy her scent.

"You are acting like you're in love!"

"Nah, kid. You're crazy. Just in deep thought."

"Yeah, I bet. Now do you want to put me on what you were talking about?"

We walked through the hallways, and right when I was about to spill the beans, I heard, "Ms. Rodriguez, we need you in the cafeteria." I turned around to hear the familiar name that Ceto mentioned. I realized that Ms. Rodriguez was the janitor lady.

Young Kaz

I turned around to look at Ceto. He smiled at me and said, "Yes, Ms. Rodriguez!" I put two and two together. Now I knew Ms. Rodriguez was whom he was talking about all along. "Look at your face, kid. Boo ya! I told you. Yo soy true Papi chulo," he said.

I nodded in disbelief, knowing I'd finally come second to Ceto, but it was cool because most of the girls he liked wouldn't give him play because they wanted me.

"Ok, you got it, kid," I told him, giving him his props.

"For real, what's up with you? You are not the same kid." Ceto said, curious to know.

"What are you talking about?"

"Vicky! I see how you look at her. Did you really beat or not? You can tell me I'm not going to say a word."

"Nah, I'm good."

"Yeah, ok. I know better, bro. I know you better than you know yourself."

While we walked the halls, I thought, *Yeah, really, what is up with me?* I knew I was falling for Vicky if Ceto could see it. I needed to pull myself together.

The day went kind of fast, but my thought process seemed kind of slow. The only thing I was thinking about was Vicky, still visualizing her face with her response about not being with Ceto. I just had this weird feeling like we were supposed to be together or something. Maybe I was just bugging out. So, as the day flowed, school was out, and I was home. I found myself lying on the bed, staring at the ceiling, waiting for some type of reaction, when suddenly I heard the phone ring. "Hello?"

"Yo, what's up, kiddo?"

"Oh, hey. What's up, Marvin? Hold on. I'm going to tell Mom you're trying to call her."

"Nah, it's cool. I just called to speak with you, if that's all right."

"Sure, what's up?"

"How did it go with Shorty?" he asked.

"I think I messed up. My boy Ceto told me he beat it already, so my intention was to handle some business with her, and that's it. For some strange reason, talking with her and hearing her voice outside of school made me want her."

Marvin laughed, then replied, "Yeah, I know how you feel, kid. It's like hearing sweet music you've never heard before that relaxes you. Oh yeah, I know that feeling! How you describe it, she sounds like she has the same qualities as your mom." As I heard Marvin explain that strange feeling, I noticed exactly what I was feeling and how I felt about Vicky.

"Word. You hit it right on the nail. The only thing is, I can't get her off my mind," I confessed.

"Trust me, kid. As much as you are thinking about her, she's thinking about you. Well, I have to go now. I just wanted to say what's up and check on you."

"Cool, thanks." After I hung up the phone, I heard the door close. I got up to see what was going on, and it was Mom. I couldn't tell if she was going or coming. "Hey, Ma!"

"Hey, baby!"

"You just getting in?"

"No, I was just kissing Marvin goodbye."

I thought to myself, *Why didn't he just knock on my door to speak to me?*

"Baby, sit down and give me a few minutes," she said.

"What's up, Ma?" I sat down, knowing the last time my mom spoke with me like this was when she told me my dad died. I did the only thing that came to my mind—brace and be ready for whatever was about to come out of her mouth.

"You know I really like Marvin a lot, right?"

"Yes?" "He stayed the night last night, and we had a serious talk about living together, but I didn't want to go through with it until I spoke with you."

Now after hearing that, I was happy. My mom didn't notice it yet because she was still breaking the news to me. She must have thought I wasn't going to like what was being said, knowing that whether I agreed or disagreed, they were going to be together regardless. I could see that my mom was happy with Marvin. And I loved the fact that she valued my opinion when it came to making a decision, especially one that she thought may affect my life.

"Yeah, Mom, sure. I'm cool with that," I said. She grabbed me as tight as she could and thanked me for allowing him to stay, as if I had a say if he stayed or went. "Ma, why didn't he just come knock on my door instead of calling?"

"He was going to, but he had to leave out for work."

I thought about what it would be like to have a man in the house for me to look up to. Although it seemed kind of scary to me, knowing my mom, she was not going to just pick anybody, so I knew for a fact he was a good man. After hearing the news, I felt good about it, and then out of the blue, I heard the phone ringing. "Ok, baby. That's all I wanted to say. Go answer your phone." She smiled, looking proud of me.

"Hello?"

"Hey, did I wake you?"

Oh my god, it was Vicky on the other line. I smiled from ear to ear, excited but keeping my cool.

"Nah, I'm up. What's up?"

"Can I come over?" I paused, not really knowing what to say. I was extremely surprised and caught off guard because we had just had a bad encounter in class, and I didn't think we would speak again. I didn't mind her coming over, so I had to man up and ask my mom if I could have company first. Maybe she would be cool about it, being that she's in a good mood, so I'd take my chances. "Oh yeah, sure. Just call me this time when you're close."

"Yeah, sure, Momma's boy." She gave a little laugh. I visualized her smiling as she said it, and I began to smile myself, but I had to wipe it quickly and come up with a game plan to see if I could persuade Mom to let me have company.

Young Kaz

I told Vicky she could come over without getting the ok from Mom. *God, please, let her say yes!*

I cried out, "Ma!"

"Yeah, baby?" I could hear her footsteps coming down the hall toward my room, and my heart started beating fast.

"Why are you yelling like you're a crazy man?"

"Can I have company today, Ma? Please, pretty please?" I pleaded. To Mom's surprise, I was a madman in love.

She looked at me and smiled. "Sure. Just make sure it's not all night. You've got school tomorrow."

Wow, I was really nervous; I thought she was going to say no. About five minutes had passed when the phone rang. "Hello?"

"It's me, Vicky."

"Yeah, I know."

"Ok, you going to open the door? I'm out front, fool."

I felt butterflies in my stomach while walking toward the door. I looked at my mom's reaction, watching me from the side, smiling while on the phone. I opened the door and saw Vicky standing there like a black queen. She had this black dress with stripes on it and a nice short jacket to cover her top. All I could say was, *damn, this girl was beautiful.* Fine butter milk chocolate skin and her hair looked smooth, black, and shiny. Her watery eyes would hypnotize you if you stared into them too long. She smelt even better than her usual candy scent as she walked in.

"What's that you have on? It's not candy."

She said, "Oh, you noticed?" with a smile. "It's called Destiny." Wow. My mouth dropped, and I thought about what me and Marvin were talking about. She just looked amazing.

"You look beautiful," I confessed.

Then my mom interrupted me to correct my response. "Boy, please. That girl looks gorgeous. Now, are you going to introduce me?" I had forgotten where I was for a split second. When I looked at my mom's face, I saw a smile, but this time, it was different.

"Yes, Vicky, this is my mom, Cynthia. Mom, this is Vicky. She goes to my school." Suddenly I heard a scream from both sides as they began to scream and greet each other with hugs and laughter simultaneously.

"Hello, Ms. Cynthia."

"Hey, girl. How's your mom doing? Tell her I said. She better call me."

I'm looking on confused, like I was singled out and forgotten about. "Someone want to explain what's going on here?" They both look at me, laugh, and continue with their conversation. They left me in suspense.

Then mom smiled at me and said, "Oh, my poor baby," while smiling. "I know Vicky's mom. That's my girl. You'll go ahead, but behave yourselves. I'm not ready to be no grandma." And Mom left us in peace. I'm still a little shocked at what just happened here. While walking toward my room, my thoughts began to race.

"Wow, I didn't know your mom was Miss Cynthia."

"Yeah, I didn't know you knew her."

"I know her well. She and my mom hang out from time to time. She's like my mom when my mom's not around. She gives me good advice."

"Your mom is mad cool. Well, I just came to get some bud." That hurt me because I really wanted her to stay. I thought she was coming over to see me. I looked at her but felt disappointed at the same time. I reached to get the bud with an attitude. "How much do I owe you, Mr. Grumpy?"

Knowing that she just wanted the bud, I just gave it to her and said she was good so she could hurry up and leave. I didn't charge her because I was disgusted with her—I wanted her to go asap. I couldn't bear to have her there another second, knowing I could not kick it with her the way I wanted.

"Ok, Mr. Nasty attitude. Thanks." She took the bud, threw five dollars down on the bed, and walked out of the room. I know it bothered me because I refused to walk her out.

I heard the door close, and my heart just fell. I went down to the kitchen to get something to drink, and to my surprise, I saw her sitting down on the couch in the living room.

"What happened? I thought you were leaving," I said with a little attitude."

"Yeah, I was."

"Well?" I reminded her.

"Well, your mom's asked me to stay for a few while she went to the store," she replied, then turned her head to watch TV.

I looked at her again, just wanting to see her smile and be closer to her. My heart was crushed, so I just walked back into my room. It wasn't long before my mom returned, and I heard the door close twice, knowing that Vicky had left.

"Kaz, come in here."

Ok, now here it comes. I know she's going to want to know what happened with us. "Yeah, Ma!"

While walking toward the kitchen, I looked into the living room to confirm that Vicky had left. "I need help with this stuff." I entered the kitchen, knowing that I was going to have to help with putting the groceries away. Then I heard my mom talking. As I entered the kitchen, I heard Vicky's voice. I stood there feeling happy but bothered at the same time—happy to see her again but bothered knowing she didn't have me on her mind. "Baby, grab those bags by the door. They're heavy."

122

"Yeah, baby. Grab those bags right there by the door," she said, taunting me. Vicky smirked while repeating after my mom, and both began to chuckle. Although Vicky looked fine as hell and sounded sweet saying it, I was still bothered, so I couldn't laugh with them. I just went to grab the bags, rolling my eyes at Vicky.

"By the way, I asked Vicky to stay over for dinner," Mom said. Honestly, all I could think about was how awkward this would be.

Young Kaz

I replied, "That's cool, Mom, but I got school tomorrow, and besides, she has to go home before it gets late."

"No, it's ok, baby. I spoke with her mother. I told her after she eats and her food has settled in, you will walk her home." Vicky looked at me and gave me a little smirk.

I picked up the heavy bags, put them on top of the table, and began walking toward my room. Suddenly, I found myself bumping into Vicky again. It felt like destiny was speaking to me because we both kind of paused, looking at each other. Just seconds after, Mom said, "Aww, puppy love," and we both turned away. I walked toward my room feeling really confused. I'd never felt this; something inside me strongly wanted her.

I heard footsteps behind me as I walked into my room, and I noticed Vicky was behind me. "Kaz, your mom told me to ask you if you want mac and cheese or Rice or Roni?" When I looked at her, I lost all control over myself because I just walked past her, closed my door, turned around, looked dead in her eyes, and just before she could say a word, I planted a huge tongue kiss on her that was so passionate she had no choice but to kiss me back. We kissed for a split second, and then she pushed me off of her.

"What's wrong with you, perv?" She stormed out of the room. I wasn't sure how she was going to take it. I began to think, *I've done it this time. By her reaction, she's either going to tell my mom and leave or just leave.*

I stayed in my room, waiting for my mom to scream at me or call me when the food was ready. I couldn't help myself. I had to get those butterflies out of my stomach. What puzzled me was that if she felt that way, why would she let me kiss her, let alone kiss me back?

"Kaz!" By the tone of her voice, I could tell I wasn't in trouble. I made my way to the kitchen to eat, but as I reached the kitchen, I saw Marvin, Mom, and Vicky sitting at the table, all three looking at me as if I had a speech in progress to explain my reaction—it was like everything went in slow motion.

I stood still, puzzled, trying to figure everyone out and their thought processes. Starting with Mom, I could already imagine what she was saying in her mind: "Aww, look at my baby, growing to be a man. We are finally a full, happy family." Marvin would be thinking, "Go ahead, champ," as he gives me a wink, co-signing his approval that Vicky was a nice catch. Now, Vicky, all I could hear was, "*You perv.*" We locked our eyes for a split second, but a second too long—long enough for my mom to burst out: "Aww! You guys, you look good together. Now that's what I call puppy love." Her outburst did just a little justice; it broke the silence at the table. After

I finished being embarrassed by Mom, I looked up at Vicky. She had this smile on her that made me feel at ease for my perv reaction.

Rickey Dudley

I wanted more than that smile. I wanted her all for myself. Just the thought of sitting next to her, listening to her sweet voice and seeing her pretty white teeth gave me butterflies, but the biggest jaw-breaker for me was when she smiled and looked me dead in my eyes. If I didn't know any better, I would say I was in love, but I didn't know what love was.

"Let's all hold hands so I can say grace."

I think I just gave away how much I was into this girl. Mom gave me a look like, '*Who the hell is at my table?*' I reached out to grab Vicky's hand. She almost hesitated, but knowing how rude that would be, she reached out. I gave her this sneaky smile, sort of saying *Gotcha*, and she gave me an eye roll.

"God is good. God is great. Thank you for this food today..." I heard chuckling underneath someone's breath, and as I opened my eyes to see where it was coming from, it seemed distant from my mom's side. Sure enough, it was—my mom was in tears, as if she'd heard the craziest joke on Earth. One thing I could say was Mom didn't sugar code anything. "Mom, now you know that's rude during prayer."

While laughing, she replied, "You're right, baby. I'm sorry. Go ahead and finish."

"I'm done. We can eat now."

"Vicky?"

"Yes, Ms. Cynthia. I see he's putting on a front for me."

"What are you talking about?" I replied.

"After your prayers, you are supposed to say amen. This must be a new type of prayer."

The whole table began to laugh. I looked over at Marvin, and my mom was cracking up in tears, although the joke was on me. I enjoyed every bit of it. Time was running out, and it was getting close to nine thirty P.M., almost time for Vicky to go home.

By the time I came out of daydreaming, Vicky was finishing up with her meal, and as I looked, Mom and Marvin were talking to each other.

"I appreciate you letting me stay over, Ms. Cynthia," Vicky said. "Anytime. You're my daughter-in-law." It's true what they say: Mom knows best. I used to hear adults say, "If you don't know if the baby is yours or not, go ask Mama. She will let you know."

I took Mom saying that she was her daughter-in-law as a sign, and with that, I reacted quickly. "Please let me get this for you." I put Vicky's plate in the sink, offering to walk her home.

She replied, "Sure, Mr. P."

"Ma, I'm going to walk her home now."

"Ok, baby. Just hurry back to get ready for school."

The moment we stepped out of the house, it happened. I found myself in a boxing match with Vicky. First, I put up my right hand to block a haymaker coming from the right, then the left, and then another right. "What the hell is wrong with you? Are you crazy, girl?"

"Just as crazy as you are, trying to pull a move like that on me!"

"What are you talking about?"

"You kissed me in your room! What did you do that for? I told you, I'm not that kind of girl."

"You're right," I told her, trying to calm her down.

"Apologize to me."

"I can't do that."

"Why not? See, you're just like the rest of them."

"My pops always said to never apologize for what you wanted to do." I walk off ahead of her to avoid another potential punch.

I heard Vicky's mouth running, "Don't walk away from me while I'm talking to you. That's rude. And why would you want to kiss me, pervert? You have a girl already. Kiss her." I know I made a crazy move by kissing her, but in the back of my mind, something was telling me to do it again. However, based on her reaction now and her not forgetting that I pulled a move on her, maybe she wouldn't want me to.

We kept walking, and I was still ignoring her, and then all of a sudden, I felt this grab, as if a lioness was about to begin feasting on its prey. Vicky grabbed me so hard and spun me around just to get my attention that I felt a pinch on my triceps. That pushed my panic button. I snatched myself away, freeing myself, which made her break her nail.

"What the fuck is wrong with you, girl? Why are you grabbing me like that?"

"I told you, I don't like when people ignore me while I'm talking." I was frustrated; I wanted her, and she wasn't giving in the way I thought she would. I gave up and just said fuck it.

"If you don't like me, why are you still worrying about the past? Just forget the shit, and let me make sure you get home. You won't have to worry about me anymore. I get the message. You don't like me." I noticed a tear fall from her eye after I snatched myself away from her. Looking into her watery eyes was the final straw for me. This girl gave me chills from how beautiful she was, and just the thought of knowing she was crying for me had me lost for words. It was like I was hypnotized, and her lips were calling. I reached in, apologizing and holding her in my arms. As I looked down, telling her how sorry I was, I noticed a little smile. It was like one of those comfort smiles. As she accepted my apology, we began to part ways. Our noses touched, and I could feel her breath. When we both went in for the kiss, that was when it happened.

An electric spark popped on both our lips, causing us to jump back from each other. We laughed so hard that we both started to tear up. I'd never experienced something so bizarre before. "See, that's God telling you to stop being nasty, perv."

We walked the short distance we had left, talking right before reaching her house. I didn't want the night to end there. I wanted to make sure that she was mine before the night ended, so I did a sucker move and I gave up my player card. "Hey, Vicky, I really enjoy being around you. I hope we can continue this."

"Of course. We peoples."

Rickey Dudley

"No, I mean, I want you to be my girl," I said with conviction.

"I like you. You are a cool friend, Kaz!"

I didn't hear a no; I heard a yes, so I went in again for another kiss, and she kissed me back again. I ended it short this time, apologizing and telling her I couldn't help it. She replied with a smile.

"I thought your daddy told you never to apologize for what you intended to do. See you later, perv." She opened her front door, giving me her back. I turned to walk away with a smile. I couldn't help but stop and turn to look just one more time, and there she was in the window, kissing me.

I couldn't think about anything else except Vicky. While walking home, my mind thought about how this night happened, and my self-esteem went through the roof. I wondered what tomorrow was going to be like.

By the time I reached the house, I saw Marvin sitting out front smoking weed. I thought to myself, *My step-pops looks cool.*

"About time, playboy. I thought you were never coming back home."

"Yeah, I almost lost. I wanted to stay with her," I said.

"Yeah, I know what you mean." He looked in toward the house, watching Mom in the kitchen window cleaning.

That was when it hit. "Could I really be in love?" I asked Marvin.

"Love is strange, Kaz, but trust and believe your heart will let you know."

"Thanks, Marvin. See you later. I'm going to bed."

"Alright. champ." While going into the house, I felt like my life was complete, and still, all I could think about was Vicky. Once I got in the house, I heard Mom, "Aww, my baby in love!"

Feeling flattered, I just smiled at Mom and replied, "Yes, I think so, Ma. Good night!"

"Ok, baby. Good night." I showered and then got under the covers, getting ready to sleep. I was so pumped with excitement that I couldn't fall asleep right away. While tossing and turning, I just decided to lie on my back and stare at the ceiling. Then t phone rang.

"Hello?" Then I heard this sweet voice on the other end.

"Just wanted to make sure you got home safe. Have a good night, baby." It sounded so sweet hearing her voice, and it made me smile.

"You too, gorgeous," I replied, then hung up the phone. I slept through the night, and then I felt this touch on my shoulder accompanied by a sweet voice that sounded familiar to me.

I turned in bed to see Vicky's face staring back at me. She proceeded to kiss me, and then I felt her hand reaching down into my boxers. Oh, yes, this was it—the moment I'd been waiting on. I did my ritual with the tip of my peter bone, rubbing it on her clit. I could feel that she was hot and ready, so I started to insert myself inside her. Then everything just went black. Suddenly, I could hear my mom in the kitchen cooking breakfast, smacking pans together. *Oh no, not now.* I tried so hard to go back to sleep, but it wasn't working.

Young Kaz

I got up to conduct my daily routine: brush my teeth, rinse my mouth with Listerine, wash my face, and freshen up. "Hey, champ!" It seemed a little strange to hear my mom call me by that name, but it was cool. The name grew on me, thanks to Marvin.

"Yeah, Mom. I'm up!"

"Oh, ok, baby. I'm heading out. Love you." When my mom left, I knew I had just about half an hour before it was time for me to go to school. *What the hell? Is that my phone ringing? It's too early for that. Maybe Mom forgot something.* I answered the phone and heard Marvin on the other end. "Hey, champ. Just making sure you're up. Your mom's left already, right?"

"Yeah, I'm up, and she just left out a couple of seconds ago," I said.

"Alright, talk with you later." I hung up the phone. I found myself looking forward to having Marvin around.

Just before I could walk away, the phone rang again. "Hello?"

"Oh yeah, grab the garbage, baby. I forgot to grab it on my way out."

"I got it. Mom, where did you put the Telenor? I've got a headache?"

"Check the bathroom cabinet."

Right after I took the Telenor, the phone rang again, and it was one I didn't really expect—Vicky. "Hey, good morning."

"Good morning. I didn't see you leave for school yet. What are you doing? Trying to cut school?"

"I'm going. I was just eating breakfast."

"Where's mine?"

"Come and get it." After I said that, I heard the phone click. I thought maybe the phone service cut us off or something happened on her end. I pressed star sixty-nine to dial back the number she called from, and it just rang. I hung up and then pressed six, nine once more, and it did the same. I hung up, thinking, *Maybe she's trying to call me while I'm calling her?* I left the receiver on the hook. The moment I did that, I heard someone knocking at the door. I recognized that knock. I opened the door to see Vicky standing there, looking good, and as the wind blew, I could smell that candy-sweet perfume on her.

I was surprised that she came over. "What's up?"

"Are you going to invite me in, or are we going to just stand here and talk?"

"My fault. Come in." I chuckled from being caught off guard. "What's going on with you? Why are you not going to school?"

"I am going to school. I wanted to walk with you to school, but I see you're not going."

"I am!"

"You're not even dressed. How do you plan on going to school in your boxers?" I stared at Vicky while she laughed. I just realized that my mind was in deep thought. I didn't even realize it, but not feeling ashamed, I looked down and laughed out loud. "Yeah, talk about easy access. Looks like I wouldn't have to do much to get some."

"Who said you were getting anything?" I replied, knowing I was starving for her inside, but I still played it smoothly. Besides, I knew she was joking.

Rickey Dudley

"Hold on just a minute. Let me jump in the shower real quick," I told her. I walked toward the bathroom while asking her a question. "Why did you want me to walk you to school?" I had this idea that came to mind that by talking to her and engaging while showering, I was luring her into the bathroom.

Within seconds, I heard her telling me, "I have to use the restroom." Talk about perfect timing. "Can you come out so I can pee?"

I thought quickly. "Come in. I'm already in the shower."

"No, please come out."

"Ok, give me a few. I've got soap on my face and in my hair."

"Ok, never mind. Just keep the curtains closed, and no peeking, perv."

"Don't worry. I won't look."

I waited for her to finish, but I couldn't help myself. I snuck and took a peek anyway, but I was too late. I caught her just in time to see her fasting up her pants. I turned the shower off, indicating that I was finishing up. "I saw you trying to look, nasty boy. I should peek in on you."

"I'm finished here. In a minute, you won't have to peek. I'm about to move this certain, and you can see it all," I said as I laughed.

I could hear Vicky calling me nasty and heard the door close. I couldn't help but laugh; I called her bluff. I decided to walk to my room with a towel on instead of getting dressed in the bathroom. I opened the bathroom door and saw Vicky standing on the side with her arms crossed with a fake mean smile. She told me she felt disrespected while looking at my chest and abs. Yeah, I couldn't lie, I started feeling myself even more, so I walked up to her like a smooth operator. I saw her take a deep breath as I walked up.

I apologized to her and grabbed her close to me with a kiss. She started breathing hard; I wanted to feel more of her. While kissing her, I was backing her up toward the bed. I slowly laid her down on my bed and slid my hands under her shirt, caressing her breasts that felt so smooth and firm. I had more than a handful. I noticed she wasn't stopping me, so I kept kissing her and lifting her shirt. I pulled her breasts out of her bra and saw their beauty. I paused at first, then I touched a nipple with my finger, moving it in a circular motion. I felt her hand lay on top of mine, and I kissed her again. Then I went to put my mouth on her breast. She inhaled and then exhaled with a nice moaning sound. "Please, stop."

I learned a lot over time by hearing the older guys talk; they would say: "Sometimes when a woman says stop, she really means keep going, and then there are times when she really means stop.

You can tell by the tone of her voice." I paid close attention to how she said stop and slowed down to see if she really meant it. I kept going because I didn't hear her say it again. I got up to reach toward the dresser drawer to get the condoms out. The towel fell, and she gave me this scared look, asking me to stop once more, so I didn't hesitate to. I was so in the mood in that moment that I would have embarrassed myself anyway. I'd never put a condom on before—shit, I'd had pussy, either. The closest I'd come to having sex was with Star, the lady in my dream.

"I'm sorry, but I'm not ready for that, Kaz."

As bad as I wanted to be inside her, I had no problem waiting until she was ready. I respected her that much. Truthfully, my hormones were just racing. I would do whatever she wanted me to do at this point. She was the only girl that I was around, and I didn't even think about sex that much.

"It's ok. No worries. I can wait until you are ready."

"Thank you! I'm sorry."

"No, don't apologize. It's ok," I said.

"Can I ask you something?"

"Sure, what is it?"

"Can I feel it?" She pointed down toward my peter bone, which was semi-soft. I walked up to her as she sat on the edge of the bed; she reached out to grab my peter bone.

"Your dick looks nice and feels good in my hand," she replied. While speaking, my peter bone was getting hard. "Oh my God, it's growing! What the fuck!" She leaned back, letting my peter bone go. I found it kind of funny, but at the same time, in my mind, I thought, *Damn, you acting like you've never seen a dick before,* assuming she was experienced already. "I didn't know they do that."

"You're funny. Why are you acting like that?"

"Acting like what?"

"Never mind."

I started to move away and put my draws back on, but she told me to wait. She reached her hand back out to grab my peter bone.

"Does that hurt? It's hard as hell, and I can see your veins," she said while squeezing it. Each time she asked, "Does this hurt?" she would squeeze harder.

"No, it doesn't, but if I don't bust a nut, it will later," I told her.

"It looks like a blow pop," she said. Then she began to jerk me off. I watched her face getting closer to the tip of my dick. I moaned and closed my eyes, just in case she was shy. I noticed she would look at me and move her face, so by me closing my eyes, she saw that I wasn't watching her. I squinted an eye open just enough to look at her every now and then, noticing she had the tip of my dick near her mouth. I could see her tongue sticking out, attempting to lick the tip.

"I don't know what's coming over me, but I really feel like putting my mouth on you." I opened my eyes in surprise at her response and told her to go ahead if she wanted—it was all hers. She looked at me and said, "I don't know where you have been putting this thing. If I do this, you belong to me only."

I told her I was already hers. She took my dick and smacked her face with a gentle touch right before licking the tip. My heart started racing at that warm feeling of my dick inside her mouth. "Did that feel good?"

"Yes, that felt great, baby," I said, encouraging her. "Ok, let me try one more thing." Hold on. Was she serious? What was this, tryouts?

Rickey Dudley

"I saw this on a porn video once. This girl swallowed the guy's whole dick." She gave it a try, but to her surprise, she couldn't do the same. She tried, but she gagged before she could get to the base, and we both began to laugh.

It came to an abrupt end with the sound of keys. *Oh shit.* "Hide in the closet," I told her. I was so nervous, thinking maybe my mom was about to walk into my room after coming into the house. I jumped in the closet with her, so now I was butt-ass naked with a hard-on, and Vicky was standing behind me. I felt uncomfortable with my ass out, literally.

She whispered in my ear, "You've got a cute butt," and then grabbed it. Before I could shout and tell her to cut the shit, she grabbed my peter bone, which made me cut my sentence short instead. She whispered again, "Turn around," and I did just that. I couldn't see what she was doing, I just felt her move, and the next thing I felt was her warm mouth around my peter bone. I couldn't believe it. I mean, I could. I just mean—shit, that felt so good. She didn't do it to completion, but hell, it was good enough for now. I had closed my eyes while she was sucking, and then I heard the door close and the key turning to lock the door. Vicky stopped.

"Come, get dressed. Let's leave while we have the chance."
I moved quickly while watching Vicky stare at me with a smile.

"What's that smile about?" I asked.

"Did you like the way that felt?"

"Sure did."

Once I got my clothes on, we left for school. The time was eleven thirty—just enough time to get to our science class. Mr. Armstrong never called home; as long as you answered during the attendance call, you were good, so being late really wasn't a problem.

We walked up to the school together, and I saw Ms. Williams staring with a little smile. "Good morning, Ms. Williams."

"Yeah, good morning, June-bug—I mean, Kaz. You want to hurry up and get to class. The bell is about to ring."

"Yeah, thanks."

"Don't thank me. Hurry up."

Me and Vicky walked into the school, and I felt a stare coming from Vicky. "Don't tell me you had sex with the security guard?"

"No, I didn't. Where are you coming from with that?"

"So, what's this June-bug thing about? Is that your nickname or something? I caught that."

I looked into her eyes while she tried to figure it out. I couldn't help but tell her the truth; besides, I wasn't hiding anything.

"Ms. Williams told me about this dude named June-bug she used to go to school with. He cut school so much that he dropped out of school at an early age. Now he's caught up in the streets doing drugs. She said if I don't shape up in school, I will be just like him. So, that's her way of telling me to shape up."

"Ok, I thought she was trying to take my man away from me."

Young Kaz

W e walked to the lockers together while talking. Our locker rooms were not too far apart, but as we reached them, we parted ways. She left me with a nice, soft kiss on the cheek. "See you later, big daddy," she said. Yeah, she boosted my ego like crazy. I watched her walk away with that fat ass of hers. Lord knew I couldn't wait to get into her pants.

I started to go into the locker room and saw Ms. Rodriguez's cart near the lockers. I played it smoothly and tried to walk by like I didn't see her. "Papi, come here, please." I thought about what Vicky said, *"You better not be sticking your thang in nothing else. You belong to me."* As I approached her, part of me was already giving in because if I gave Ms. Rodriguez some, she wouldn't know anyway.

"Yes, what is it?"

"Papi, can you pick up this gym bag for me and put it on top of the locker so I can mop this side." I damn nearly struggled with it myself, but I still managed to lift the bag on top of the locker. Then I thought to myself, *Should I bust a nut or wait for Vicky?* "Thank you, Papi!"

"You're welcome." With no hesitation, I headed toward my classroom.

Coming to school now felt awkward, sitting in class with Vicky in front of me and not being able to touch her the way I wanted. It was cool, though, because it made me want her more. Every little thing she was doing turned me on further. Every now and then, I would see her turn around and give me a smirk, as if only me and her knew our little secret of wanting each other.

It felt good. One stare became two, and by the third, we locked eyes, as if we were trying to read each other's minds. It wasn't long before we got interrupted by none other than, yes, Ceto. He busted into the classroom, making everyone laugh as usual while dancing and singing his own anthem song.

While reading my assignments, Ceto and I began talking at the back of the class. "Can y'all keep it down back there? People are trying to work," Vicky said with a smile that quickly turned into a frown because of Ceto.

"Sure, my Chula. Papi got you." We both began to laugh.

"What's up, bro? How was your weekend?"

"My weekend was whack, bro. Mom moved to this new neighborhood. Shit is whack, bro. It takes me longer now just to get to school, but fuck that. Bro, guess what? Remember Nadine?"

"Yeah, shorty with the fatty," I replied.

"I beat that this weekend."

"I thought you'd been hitting that," I said, confused.

147

"Nah, bro, last time I didn't finish. I was going to hit the culo, but she wasn't with that."

"Oh shit, my guy finally got some pussy." I was happy for him, but I now felt he had one up on me. I was still a virgin, I didn't even know what it felt like, but I'd be damned if I let Ceto know that. "Yeah, bro. I was aiming for the culo, like toma eso mama! She moved like a pro, bro! I went to spread her culo cheeks and stick it in, but she just moved up and did this crazy bend, and I fell right inside her womb."

"About time you got some pussy, bro," I told him, sounding proud.

"I like ass better, bro. It's tighter, and I heard it helps get your monster bigger," said Ceto.

"Yeah, and it helps you get smarter, too," I replied sarcastically.

"I knew it, bro! That's why I have been acing my grades." We looked at each other and just burst out laughing. I didn't know why he was laughing, but I was laughing because of Ceto. Either he really believed what I was saying, or he was responding with sarcasm too.

"Quiet down in the back. The class is working. If y'all don't want to share what y'all are talking about, keep it down. Better yet, get out of the class." The class turned toward us, expecting to fill them in on what we were talking about, but we ignored them and

148

kept quiet. Vicky turned to look at me again, and we locked eyes again. I looked at the clock because I couldn't wait until the day was over so I could hold her.

"Yo, stop staring, girl. Damn! Turn around and do your work."

"Ceto, chill. It's cool. I like when she stares." Vicky gave me this surprising stare as if she was proud of me for sticking up for her. I had no choice—that was my baby, and Ceto still didn't know we were seeing each other. I wasn't sure if I should say anything just yet, but I was sure my actions gave it away because normally, me and Ceto would crack jokes on her. I was in a dream world, staring back and smiling at Vicky. By the time I finished my sentence, I had looked back at Ceto, and I laughed out loud because of the face Ceto was making. You know, like when a dog looks at you sideways when you mimic him howling? Yes, that look, like, what the fuck are you doing?

We cut the talking out and got back to our work. I noticed Vicky got up to go to the bathroom. When she got up, I lifted my head to watch her walk. "What's up with you?" Ceto said.

"What are you talking about?"

"Am I missing something with you and Vicky?" I watched as she went out the door to make sure the coast was clear.

"Yeah, bro. I'm digging her. I'm going to ask her out soon. Just waiting for the right time," I said to see how he would respond.

He was cool about it, mostly. "Damn, bro. I can't diss her anymore. It's cool, though, because if you do mess with her, she's going to be my sister-in-law, and I can still crack ass on her, just respectfully now."

"We are not getting married, bro!"

Young Kaz

The moment I said that, she walked into the classroom and looked dead at me while walking to her seat. Damn, this girl had it going on. I stared and thought for a moment, *Yeah, I could see myself married to her.*

We had about fifteen minutes left of the class, which still felt like an eternity, but it was winding down. "Yo, I meant to tell you, remember them fools that jumped you?" said Ceto.

"Yeah, what's up?"

"I saw one of them. He didn't do shit, though. He just looked at me and smiled, looking like a dickhead."

"Where at?"

"In the new area where I moved to out in Brooklyn. I saw him when I was going into the store."

"Damn, bro. Why did your mom move so far and out of all places, Brooklyn?"

"Yeah. I know, right?"

Within minutes, the bell rang, and we all proceeded to our next classes. Before going to my locker, I walked Vicky to hers. I was making it known that we were together; neither side was hesitant. I sent her off to class with a see-you-later kiss. Then I was off to the locker room to get dressed to ball.

While getting dressed, my mind started to wonder about June-bug. *What is June-bug doing right now? I wonder how he looks.* I doubt he saw himself becoming homeless or being on drugs in the future. What steps was he taking when he saw it coming, or did he not see it?

I fell into a deep daydream but quickly came out of it, thanks to Ceto. "Yo, my dude, I'm not going to hit the gym today. I'm leaving with Nadine." Now normally, Ceto and I chilled together, but our paths had changed because we both had girls now. They weren't lying when they said a woman could change a man's direction. I thought, *Why play ball when I can go chill with Vicky?* But then again, I didn't want to be around her and her friends, so I did what any player would do. I decided to go bust some ass by myself. Not to brag, but I was good either way on the basketball court—with or without a team.

I got down in a game of twenty-one with the other fellas in the gym so I could test my skills just to see how good I was. I'm not going to lie, I was showing my ass off; shit, I was flying like Michael Jordan and breaking kneecaps like Allen Iverson.

I heard in the background, "That's my baby out there winning. Come on, baby! You got this!" Hearing Vicky cheer me on gave me a mean ego boost, so I went for the dunk.

I was about to dunk it on this buster, but out of nowhere, I heard this crawl followed by a block, which caused me to miss the dunk and land on my ass. "You motherfucker! Why did you do that to my baby?"

Rickey Dudley

Vicky was yelling at this kid at the top of her lungs. *Shit, if no one knew we were messing around, they did now.* While sitting on my ass, I saw the dude coming toward me, flexing and proud of himself for stopping my dunk. He gave me a look of *Not around here, buddy.* I couldn't front—he got that one off, though. He stretched his hands out to help me up, and I gave him that look like, *I got this, boy—you need more than that to stop me from winning.* I got up, shook it off, and gave him a smack on the ass for stopping that dunk. When I got the basketball again, man, oh man... I left him on the floor by breaking his ankles, followed by a nice dunk, leaving my cheerleaders shouting with joy and me swinging like an ape on the rim.

After ending the game with that fast break and dunk, I went over to him and stretched my hand out to help him up with a smile, and we both started laughing. Afterward, I went over to Vicky to get my victory kiss. That kiss said a lot, making it official to her that I didn't care if people knew about us.

We kissed once more, and the next thing I knew, I heard, "Calmate, Mommy. Your tongue is in my brother's throat, and he can't breathe." I had been around Ceto long enough to know just a little Spanish, so you know I had to show off. Vicky looked at me with a confused look, so I decided to educate her.

"Calmate means to calm down, but I don't want you to."

"Ok, Papi," was her reply. It sounded different to the way she said it, but it was funny and sexy.

"Ceto, what's good, bro? Did you see it? Tell me you saw how I cracked your boy's ankles and then smashed it on him," I carried on.

Young Kaz

I wasn't sure what was happening to me and Ceto, but we'd calmed down a lot, especially in school. We started taking school seriously, and we would only have fun during lunchtime or gym. Ceto managed to keep Nadine, and my sweet Vicky was never too far away from me. You could say it all worked out in our favor: Ceto finally scored with Nadine, and I kept my promise to Ms. Williams about staying focused and succeeding in school—in other words, not becoming another June-bug.

As time passed, Mom was happy Marvin and I had gotten closer. When I started calling him Pops, his face would light up. Our time at school was at hand, our last year, finally the twelfth grade— not sure how we made it, but we all did. I guess you could call us the Fantastic Four. We all had our plans in order. Ceto and I still had a love for basketball and planned on getting a scholarship for a team in college.

As for Nadine, she became my sister. I looked out for her whenever Ceto wasn't around, and vice versa. Nadine's goal was to become a lawyer, and Vicky's goal was to become a teacher, plus my wife in the future. I never thought I'd talk like that so early, but I felt complete.

Now here we were, the "Fantastic Four" at lunchtime, doing what we did best: having fun. But today would be one of the days

I'd never forget. Mr. Hill, our principal, was the coolest. I think anyone would love to have him as their principal. He took over during my term in the twelfth grade. At first, he was anal, but it was just his way of getting to know the students and staff.

Anyhow, I was telling a joke that had half of our table laughing. You could say our table was the most popular with a basketball star, like me, and my crazy sidekick. We started cracking jokes on people at our table; no one was exempt—shit, we even cracked jokes on our girlfriends too.

Vicky got a little bothered and threw a piece of cake at me. I thought she was mad, and I looked down at the cake that messed up my T-shirt and then at Vicky and saw her smiling. I did the only smart thing anyone would do. I threw a piece back at her, and it splattered on her face and hair. Ceto started laughing, and right before he could catch his breath, Vicky threw a piece of cake in his face. Nadine started laughing, and with no hesitation, Ceto threw cake in Nadine's face and jumped on the table like a madman, screaming like Scarface. "Come on, you want to play rough? Ok!"

Before you knew it, he yelled the sacred words that would possess everyone in the lunchroom: "FOOD FIGHT!" as little pieces of cake fell from his face.

No sooner than he said that, you heard an echo in the lunchroom of everyone yelling, "Food fight!" Food began flying all over the lunchroom. Me and Vicky got under the table to avoid being bombed on with food, then we looked at each other and gave each other a kiss before going back into war. Me and Vicky ganged up on Ceto and Nadine, but there was just one problem: the last piece of cake I had in my hand was a big piece.

It had already released it in the air and was in slow motion, heading toward Ceto. But it just missed him; the cake continued to fly through the air like in a movie. The lunchroom stopped on impulse, and everyone just stared at Mr. Hill. *Pow!* Right in his face. The only thing I thought was, *Damn, whose house can I stay at now because there's no way I'll be able to go home and face Mom with this one?*

Mr. Hill had a bad look on his face. If looks could kill, the whole lunchroom would have been dead.

Rickey Dudley

I thought he was a psycho for a minute because he started to smile, and then the unthinkable happened. Mr. Hill yelled, "Food fight!"

I couldn't believe it. I thought I was dreaming until a mushy banana hit me in the face that Mr. Hill had thrown. I wish I could've recorded this moment—no one would believe me. The principal was in a food fight with students.

Suddenly, Mr. Hill spoke on the bullhorn, "Alright, alright, y'all. Let's cut this lunch break short so we can get cleaned up and ready for the next class. Those that have gym, head straight there, and the rest of you get to your locker room and clean up the best way y'all can without any playing. Then go straight to your next classes!"

When the bell rang, everyone was back to work like nothing ever happened. That was the best time I'd ever had in school—well, besides meeting Ms. Rodriguez. My last year of high school was turning out pretty well. The only thing that changed was mine and Ceto's time schedules; we only saw each other if we went to the bathroom by coincidence, I popped up and checked on him in his class or vice versa, and lunchtime. I stayed on my grind with schoolwork. Ceto was slacking, I guess, because I wasn't there to keep him in check. I know Ceto; he had to fit in, and the only way of doing that was by being the class clown.

I happened to see Vicky at the door, waving for me to come out of the classroom. "Hey, baby, sorry to pull you out of class, but I wanted to know, can we go out tonight, maybe a dinner and a movie?"

"Sure. Is that why you pulled me out of class? That could have waited."

"I just wanted to give you a kiss. That's the real reason." As I kissed her, I realized the kiss was the most passionate kiss we'd had since that first night we kissed. Before the teacher came to the door, I was already on my way back in the classroom to hear a bunch of oohs and awws from my classmates as well as the teacher, but it was cool; everyone got along with me. Even the teacher understood mine and Vicky's crazy love for each other. So now I planned to see what movie we were going to watch and what restaurant.

I continued to write the rest of the work off the board just in time before the bell rang. I got my books and headed toward my locker. I thought it was strange that I didn't see Ceto, as we always bumped into each other around this time.

As I rumbled into my locker, putting some books away and taking some out, I saw Ceto coming down the hallway. I lit up just for a little bit with a smile, happy to see my brother, but my smile went away and turned into a frown as he got closer. I could see that his left eye had a knot on it.

"What the fuck happened to you?"

"Nothing. I'm good, bro. Mom caught me selling weed. She hit me with a hard ass yellow bat a few times, but that last hit caught me in the face."

"Damn, Moms went Darryl Strawberry on your ass." I laughed so hard, but in the back of my mind, I just couldn't understand why this dude came to school like that and had the nerve to be happy. "Yo, Ceto, why did you come to school, kid? I would've stayed home so no one could see that shit. It looks like you have three eyes."

"Yeah, I know, but it makes me look gangster. Watch this." I was watching to see if he was going to pull some kind of trick, but as I turned around, I saw Nadine coming up behind me.

"Hey, Kaz, hey, ba—" Before she could even get "baby" out, she turned into this raging but nurturing woman I'd never seen before. "Who did this to you, baby? I'm going to kick their ass," she said, rubbing Ceto's face.

The look on Ceto's face was priceless. He looked like a puppy, and you could tell he loved every bit of it. *Strange guy, I tell you.* "I'm ok, baby. You know they couldn't hold me down. I managed to knock three of them out, but the other three got the best of me," he said, believing his lie. As he told her this bogus ass story, he looked at me and winked with his good eye, walking away smiling with Nadine babying him. I continued laughing and turning toward my locker when I paused. I saw this sticker on my locker, which read:

Hello,

I've been watching you for some time now, and I see how you treat your girlfriend. She's lucky to have you, but I want some of what she's getting, and when I get you, I'm going to suck you until your toes curl.

P.S. See you soon.

Your secret admirer.

I heard footsteps, making me react fast, crumpling up the note in time. I was puzzled.

"Hey, baby, what you up to?" Vicky asked.

"Oh, nothing. Just about to go to my last class for the day."

"Ok, love you. I'm heading to mine now. I'll be at your house around seven."

"I'll be waiting." This was just creepy, not knowing who was watching me. After I left Vicky, I went to my last class for the day, which went by kind of quickly. Now I found myself going to my gym locker. I put all my books inside so I could be ready for tomorrow, and I didn't have any homework. I heard a voice. "Hello, is there anyone in here?"

"Yes. I'm leaving now," I replied. I walked towards the door and noticed the voice was Ms. Rodriguez. Wow, she aged beautifully. "Oh my God, Kaz! Wow, you got big. I almost didn't recognize you." She reached out to hug me. She held me so tight; I didn't want her to let go. She felt good in my arms.

"Well, you know I can't stay young forever."

"Yeah, you're right. I'm so proud of you." In my mind, I was thinking about going for another round. "I see someone's almost done with school. That's a good thing. Keep it up. You can do it. Nice seeing you again. I got to get back to work."

"Same to you, take care," I said. While I was walking away, I looked back only to see her bending over, ass spread wide in her work clothes. I had to let her know I was watching her. "See you later, Ms. Rodriguez," I replied with a little flirtation to it. She waved her butt from side to side, still bent over, reaching her hand out to wave with a smile.

I wasn't expecting that, but she made me laugh. While leaving school, I realized I was almost the last person leaving, and then I saw a woman walking away from the gate of the school. I stopped and watched as she had spandex on. They were tight in her ass, not wedgie-tight, but you could say they fit her like a second skin. She had on a one-piece spandex that fits the whole body, and her body was nicely shaped. Now I loved me some Vicky, but I hadn't had sex with her yet, and my hormones took over.

I walked up to her and grabbed her hand. I threw a quick five-dollar bill on the floor for backup. I said, "Excuse me, miss. Hold up. You dropped something."

As she turned around, she replied, "Nigro, if you don't—" She paused, looking at me.

I paused, too, then used my backup. "You dropped your money on the floor." I went to pick it up for her, and she quickly took it out of my hand and stuffed it in her bra with a smile. "Can I get a name with that smile?"

"My name is Joy." I watched her as she walked away with a smile. Then it hit me. *Damn, Vicky. Let me hurry up and get home.* Just before reaching home, I stopped by the store to get some Bob Marley paper and a Phonte leaf to roll my bud.

By the way, Mom was letting me smoke now. She figured I was doing my thing in school, and it didn't have a negative effect on me, so it was cool as long as I smoked in my room and not outside. While going inside, Mom and Marvin were sitting in the living room, cuddling and watching a movie. "Mom, Pops, what's up?"

"Hey, baby. How was school?"

"Ok. Can't wait until it's over for good."

"Have you decided what college you want to go to yet?" asked Marvin.

"Not yet."

The phone rang, so that meant I got home just in time to catch Vicky's call. "Peace. Who's this?" was my new way of answering the phone.

"This is big perm, fool. Where's my money?" It was Vicky playing around.

"Hey, baby girl. What movie do you want to see?"

"I was thinking I could come over?" Asking my mom for company wasn't a problem at the age of twenty; it was just out of respect.

Young Kaz

Ma, Vicky coming over!" I yelled, too lazy to get up.

"Hush, boy. I don't care," she yelled back.

"Did you have to yell? That was my ear, fool."

"My bad."

"I'm on my way. Be there in a few." While she was getting ready, I was rolling my weed up and pumping my music. I was interrupted by a call.

"I need you. Can you stop by the school real quick?" asked Ceto.

"Say less. I'm on my way right now!" With no hesitation, I rushed out to check on Ceto.

"Mom, I'll be right back. Tell Vicky not to leave. I'm going to the store."

"Ok!" I rushed out the door toward the school, which was not that far from my house. I saw Ceto standing on the corner, and he seemed ok.

I looked around to canvas the area, and nothing, so I calmed my nerves down and approached him. "What's up? What we doing?" If you didn't know, 'what we doing' is like our code for saying, 'I'm down for whatever.'

"My bad, bro, but I was scared. I needed someone."

"Talk to me, man. What's up?"

"Well, I got this dude coming now to pick up two ounces of weed. I need you to be my hitman."

"Dude, are you serious? I don't even have a gun."

"Yeah, but he doesn't know that. All you've got to do is just play the role. If he looks like he's about to move funny, just put your hand under your shirt like you're about to pull out on him." The things we do for love... Like I said, that was my brother, so I had his back until the end.

Just before I could reply, the car rolled up on us, and I turned around quickly like I was about to draw, reaching under my shirt like Ceto said. Then I heard, "Hold on, youngblood. I'm not the enemy. Ceto, get in."

Ceto responded quickly, "I'm good, papa." He walked to the side of the car while making a hand exchange: money for the weed.

"Thanks, young blood. I'm going to get right tonight. Oh, and Ceto, tell your man to calm down. He's going to scare your customers away," the stranger replied. While he pulled off, Ceto and I looked at each other and began laughing.

Before I could say a word, Ceto replied, "I'm really sorry, bro. I didn't mean to call you for that, but I had to think quickly while he was on his way. I thought they were going to try to rob me."

"It's cool, bro."

"No, it's not. Brothers aren't supposed to put brothers in harm's way. I was scared. But on another note, you're going to be an uncle, bro. Yeah, Nadine is pregnant. She's two weeks," he said.

"Congrats, brother! You good now, though, because I got Vicky coming over?"

"Yeah, yeah. Thanks, bro. We can talk about this later."

"Alright. I'll kick it with you later."

Rickey Dudley

Walking off and heading home, I began to think about having a real gun. That feeling of being the man and just thinking about how homeboy froze? Yeah, that felt good.

I rushed toward the door, thinking Vicky should be here by this time. "Ma, did—"

Before I could finish, I heard Vicky's voice. "Yeah, I'm here. Where have you been, mister?" I looked surprised, and Mom and Pops looked at me while smirking.

"Oh, I see what this is. Y'all ganging up on me again. Not this time." In a playful manner, I gave chase toward Vicky, and before I could grab her, my mom moved like a superwoman and jumped on my back. I fell to the floor and noticed Vicky coming back like a mean bull, shocking me right in the gut.

Now my boy Marvin reacted. He grabbed my mom off me and began tickling her. I bounced up and chased Vicky into my bedroom. Somehow, Mom was right back on my back, so now all three of us started wrestling, me, Mom, and Vicky, but I said to myself, *Wait, where the hell is Marvin?* "Wow, Pop. Really? You're going to just stand by the door and watch?"

"You never tagged me in, son." He watched with a smile.

"Really? I'm trying to get them off me. I need help!"

"Oh, now I can come into your room?"

As he rushed inside, I thought, *Ok, I'm good now,* but he grabbed me down, and all of them started tickling me.

"Alright, mercy!" I pleaded. "Pops, you sold me out!" He and Mom laughed while exiting, leaving me and Vicky breathing heavily.

"Wow, I would love to stay here with y'all. My family is nothing like this. Your father is crazy cool."

I paused because I wanted to say, "He's not my father," but so far, that was all he'd been to me since Mom brought him into my life. "Yeah, he's cool. He's my Step Pops."

"Oh, sorry!"

"It's ok. He's been real good to me. I can't think of anyone else to take my dad's place."

"Can I ask you something?"

"Sure, what is it?"

"What were you and Ceto doing on that corner?"

"You saw me!"

"Dah?"

"Just talking. He said Nadine is two weeks pregnant."

"What? And she didn't tell me!"

"Don't say anything. He just found out."

"Ok, so what are we going to watch?"

170

"Don't know yet."

"Kaz, y'all want to watch Love Jones with us?" Mom yelled from the living room.

"Really? Y'all don't believe in just going to get the other person? Y'all just yell at each other."

"Alright, Mom!" I yelled back, being funny toward Vicky.

She reached out to punch me in the chest for yelling next to her ear—you could say it was a love tap. Me and Vicky went to the living room, and I went to get the drinks. Mom already had the popcorn busting it down. She and Marvin were so into the movie they almost bit their fingers off. I sat next to Vicky on the floor.

Young Kaz

I enjoyed every moment. I felt so good inside that I couldn't even describe it to you. You could just say it was a high I'll never forget.

We heard a hard knock at the door. We all looked disturbed, and before I could get up, Marvin was already at the door. "How can I help you, young man?"

"Hello, sir, my name is Mick. Is Vicky here? I'm her brother."

"Vicky, your brother Mick is at the door for you," Marvin replied. We both got up quickly, Vicky to see why her brother was at the door, and me, well, I finally got to see how he looked. I always heard that voice, but now I got to see what his face looked like. "What's up?"

"Mom is going to Atlantic City tonight, and she won't be back until tomorrow. She told me to tell you if you're going to come home, don't come home too late, but if you want to stay the night, let her know. If you're not, I'll give you the keys."

"You're going to be home, right?"

"No, I'm going to my baby mom's house. Hold on, is this Mr. Kaz that's dating my baby sister?" said Mick.

"Yes, sir. She's my baby," I said confidently.

"That's cool. Make sure she's safe."

"Will do!" I said.

"I know, because I'm going to hold you accountable."

"Hold on, let me ask Ms. Cynthia."

"Ms. Who?" asked Mickey.

"Cynthia, you remember her when we use to live in Harlem? She was the lady next door that used to babysit us."

"Oh shit, let me see her." He rushed in between us without an invite. I was amazed because the gangster went out, and you saw the little kid come out of him when he heard my mom's name.

"Ms. Cynthia…" he said softly.

"Yeah, how can I—oh shit, come here, boy. Where the fuck have you been?" She hugged him, embracing him as if he was her lost son. Throughout this year, I've learned something new multiple times about my mom's history that always seemed to amaze me.

"I'm cooling, Auntie. I have a little kid now. He's ten years old."

"Wow. I hope you stay out of trouble."

"Yes, I am. I'm about to go see my little one now. Just checking on Vicky because my mom is going to Atlantic City, and she won't be back until tomorrow. I'm staying the night," he said.

"No sweat. I got her for the night."

"Ok, nice seeing you, Auntie."

"Don't be a stranger. You know where to find me now."

As Mickey started to head out, he looked at me with a head nod, as if to say, '*Let me holla at you.*'

"Mick…" said Vicky."

"It's cool. I just want to talk to him."

"It's cool, baby. Let me talk to my brother-in-law," I said confidently.

"Oh, that's how you are giving it up with my sister?" he said.

"Yup."

"That's cool, but check this out. Your boy almost got dealt with. You need to holla at him and tell him to slow down," he whispered.

Rickey Dudley

What do you mean?"

"Your boy, Ceto. I was in the back seat of the car not too long ago with the tinted windows. I had the gun aimed at his ass. The only reason I didn't shoot him was because I saw you."

"I don't understand. This is the first time we are seeing each other," I said.

"Well, this is not my first time seeing you except in person. I see you almost every day when I'm checking on Vicky." I looked puzzled. "Your picture, man. Seeing a picture of you in her room. Anyway, take care, bro. Oh, give her these keys to the house for me."

He walked away, and I was surprised Vicky had a picture of me in her room. As I locked the door, I put two and two together. Wow, if she had never put my picture in her room, me and Ceto probably would have been dead.

I looked at her with joy, without her knowing that she saved my life, and I saw her smile. The night was ending, and everyone was getting sleepy.

"Kaz, fix the bed for Vicky and get your blanket."

"Ma!"

"Oh, you thought y'all was sleeping in the bed? No, baby!" she said. I was mad. Shit, I wanted to sleep with her in my arms and, of course, try to get a little bit.

While looking at Vicky, she began to laugh at me, whispering, "Nasty boy." I got Vicky set up in my bedroom and fixed the couch for myself.

It was so quiet in the house; you could tell everyone was asleep. I thought about going inside my room and thanked the movie "Love Jones" for giving me the idea. There was a part when Larenz Tate had to sleep on the couch, and he decided to go upstairs inside his girlfriend's room, so I did exactly that.

"Vicky, you up?" I whispered.

"Yeah." I crawled into the bed with just my boxers on. I noticed she was just in her panties. I held her close, her skin next to mine, and we both started breathing heavily. I couldn't help myself; I leaned in for a kiss. We started kissing passionately as I slid down to her breasts. I was licking around her nipples, and then I began to nibble on them, and hearing her moan made me harder. I felt her hand caressing my peter-bone. *Oh man, I have the meanest hard-on right now.*

"Come here, baby. Get on top," I told her. I was ready for her to put me inside her. As she got on top, I felt her taking my dick, moving it around on her private area and moaning. I went to help her, sliding her panties to the side. Now the tip of my dick was massaging her lips, hearing her moan more.

Right before I started to put the head in, she stopped me and said, "I'm not ready. Sorry." She went to lay on the side, depressed.

"It's ok, baby. You don't have to be sorry," I consoled her. "I'm sorry, Kaz, but thanks for waiting. Can I just do something else for now?"

"Sure," I said. Who the fuck was I kidding? I was getting blue balls and was dying to get inside her. I was about to go crazy already. "What do you want to do?" I asked.

She looked me in the eyes and then crawled to the end of the bed. "Stand over here," she said. I responded to her command; she pulled my boxers down, causing my penis to bounce, hitting her in the face.

She grabbed my penis, and away she went, putting it in her mouth. I damn near buckled as she began sucking and licking around the tip. "Oh shit," I replied as it got better. I looked down to see she was enjoying this as much as I was. She did it for a good twenty minutes, and I didn't bust, but I was ok with that. She went to kiss me right after, and with no hesitation, I kissed her back. I figured it was my dick, so why not kiss her? Besides, I didn't bust. Yeah, I'm in the safe zone. I went back to the couch, feeling at ease. Let's just say it was good enough for me to fall asleep.

Young Kaz

When I woke up the next morning, I noticed my chest feeling a little heavy and the sound of Mom cooking in the kitchen.

I tried to adjust my eyes to see better. "Aww, y'all look cute," said Mom. Before I could say a word, I noticed Vicky was sleeping on my chest, and she had my shorts and t-shirt on.

"Good morning, Ms. Cynthia!"

"Good morning, baby! I got y'all breakfast here when y'all ready." I got up to do my daily norm, and I was in the bathroom brushing my teeth when Vicky came along, brushing hers. *Guess she found my extra toothbrush.* "Can you walk me home? I'm not sure if Mick is there or not. It's too early for Moms to be home. She's a true party pooper for real. I'm not expecting her until noon time," Vicky said.

"Of course. Right after we eat, we can head straight out," I told her.

After we took care of our hygiene, we ate some good old scrambled eggs and cheese with cheese grits, turkey sausage, and garlic toast. Then we gathered our things to head toward Vicky's house, and she held my hand while walking.

"Kaz, you know I love you, right?" she said with emotion.

"Sure, I love you too, big head, but don't start getting all mushy on me. My mom's food has that effect!" We laughed.

While walking, Vicky realized she didn't have the keys. "Aww fuck. Damn, Mick, he's not home, and he didn't even leave me the keys."

"Don't worry. I'll save the day," sounding like a superhero.

"Boy, are you crazy? If you break this door or window, I'm telling on that ass."

"I do this for a living," I said while laughing as I proceeded to open the door, convincing her, as if I'd broken into homes before.

I wiggled the door and pushed three times, putting on a front. Looking at her face, she really thought I was going to break in. I just pulled the keys out of my pocket and smiled. "See, I told you. No sweat, I got you."

"Yeah, you had me for a minute. Now move out the way, fool, and give me my keys." Vicky grabbed her keys and shoved me to the side right before going in. "Come inside and have a seat. Give me a few minutes, ok? I want to take a quick shower."

"Sure, I'll wait right here!"

"You can help yourself to something to drink or snacks if you like."

She walked into her room to prepare herself to take a shower, and I did what any person would do—I followed her to her room. "Ok, I see you, Sister Soldier." She had a Black Power picture of

Malcolm X, and my picture was right on the same side. "Now I got to ask this question—who is this handsome gentleman right here next to Malcolm X?" referring to myself.

"Oh, him? That's my husband. He's inspiring, intelligent, strong, and sexy," she replied.

I'm not going to lie, I was gassed up. I made a mental note of all these positive attributes she was giving me. She began to pull her shirt off and then her bra. *Oh man, look how those beautiful things, just sitting up waiting for me to suck them*, I thought.

She's about to take her panties off right in front of me, I tell myself. I looked at her body as she walked toward me and kissed me. "Baby, be out in a minute," she said. After our quick kiss, I literally watched her ass walk right by me. After about a minute or so, I heard, "Kaz, can you bring me that pink rag on my dresser?" I grabbed the rag, walked into the bathroom, and, man, I was amazed. I paused as I watched her rub the bar of soap on her beautiful body, soap suds dripping off her nipples and between her legs. The guys in school would have loved to be in my shoes right now. This strange thought of sucking her pussy came across my mind as I looked at the soap suds on her pussy lips.

"Damn, you beautiful," I said while handing her the rag.

"Thanks, baby, I'll be out in a few." I took the liberty of roaming the house, and then I went back to Vicky's room. I expected her room to look dirty—you have some girls that looked good as hell, and their rooms be looking like a tornado hit it. Unfortunately, Vicky's room was good, check. Now the room I really wanted to see was Mick's, I walked up to one door, and right before I could turn the knob, I smelled the scent of weed coming from another door. Yup, jackpot, this was her mom's room here, so the other one over here had to be Mick's. I pushed the door open slightly, just in case, and saw a statue of a naked black man. What the fuck? This was her mom's room; I was caught off guard.

I was about to leave, but then I went back to the other door and opened it, and there it was: a baby picture of Mickey and Vicky with their mom. His room was very scary, all that thug shit, how he looked and dressed. If you were to see his room, it didn't match his thuggish style. There were no pictures or anything to tell you what type of person he was. No hints from books to give you an idea of how he thought or perceived life. I'd had enough. I closed the door, and by the time I sat down, Vicky was coming out of the bathroom dressed up. She had this long black dress on with a white design in it, and her hair was straight with a nice bracelet charm on her wrist. I'm glad I have her as my queen.

"Let's go. I'm ready, and yes, I know my brother is a weirdo. I know you saw his room."

"Nah, I didn't."

"You want to see?"

"Nah, I'd rather go to school. We're going to be late if we don't head out now," I said.

Rickey Dudley

At school, I gave Vicky a kiss, and we parted ways. I had to go to the gym locker to get my books before going to class. Guess who I bumped into right before going into the gym locker room, none other than Joy. It caught me off guard because I thought she was just passing by the school. I'd never seen her here. It would be bad for Vicky to catch me, but I had to say something so I could move on.

"Hey, stranger," I said in a friendly voice.

"Oh, hey, Kas."

"Nah, it's Kaz, with a z."

"Kaz, my bad!" she said.

"I didn't know you went here. I've never seen you here before," I said curiously.

"That's because you haven't been very observant."

"Right, anyway, nice seeing you," I said. As I tried to brush her off and get to class, she gave me this look like she wanted to eat me. I was flattered, but I belonged to Vicky, and I was not trying to fuck that up. Right before I could pass her, she grabbed my ass, winked at me, and walked away. At that moment, I knew I had to be on guard with this girl.

Now that I had my books, I was set for my classes. First, second, and third classes were done, and now was lunchtime.

"Alright, listen up. I just want to thank all of you for yesterday. I had the time of my life and my dream came true of having a food fight with my students. Now y'all know I love y'all, and I don't mind if y'all have fun, but no more food fights, ok? I had to pay overtime to the staff to clean up and for their hard work in making the food. Some of the staff were upset with me. I apologized for the food fight, and I took the blame. Understand, everyone, to some of you, this is your last year. I wanted y'all to have something to remember, and with that, thank y'all once again. Carry on!" said Mr. Hill.

He left a big impact on me, and I'll never forget that moment. I sat down at the table with Ceto, Nadine, and Vicky and began to think about Joy. We all ate, laughed, and cracked a couple of jokes as usual, and right after our lunch, we walked the hallways toward our lockers.

"I'll be back. I'm going to the restroom," said Vicky.

"Wait for me for me, girl. I got to go to," Nadine followed.

"Snap out of it, bro. You in a daze," Ceto replied.

As soon as I snapped out of my daze, I saw a note on my locker. It read: "Roses are red, violets are blue. I bet you want to know who's leaving this note for you. P.S. Love you."

"What's that about?" Ceto asked.

"I have no clue, bro," I said, looking confused.

"You haven't been fucking with anyone else, right?"

"Not at all. I just made one move but didn't really follow it through. I came to my senses quick."

"Well, I don't think that person came to theirs. From the looks of that note, they want you bad, brother, but do something quick with that note because here come the girls."

"What do you think, bro? Should I tell her?"

"Tell her what? About that note that has some words on it that end with saying I love you? I don't know about that one, bro."

"Nadine, I slipped a note inside Kaz's locker. I want to see how he's going to react," said Vicky.

"Why would you do that?"

"Just being romantic. Some boys like that when you write them letters."

"I'll think I'll try that with Ceto one day. Shit, he probably wouldn't even read it. He might just throw it in the trash knowing him," said Nadine.

"You good, bro, getting love notes and shit. We already have to do a lot of reading in school. I would've just trashed that shit," said Ceto. Ceto and I laughed, but time was running out because the girls were closing in on us, and then, out of all days, I saw Joy walking toward me. *What am I going to do?* Vicky and Nadine were getting closer, and Vicky looked like she was walking right up on me.

I felt claustrophobic, but it was too late. The girls were here, and I didn't want to look up because I knew Joy would be nearby. On impulse, I went to hug Vicky, and before I could get any closer to her, Joy was right between us. "Oh, excuse me, you love birds." She gave me a stare and continued to walk past us. I looked puzzled; I was stuck and didn't know what to do.

I knew that note was in my pocket, and I had to trash it. I was still not sure if I should tell Vicky or not. Vicky then said, "Did you get my note?"

I looked at Ceto with a sign of relief, and I was about to dig in my pocket to show her I received it. She reached to open my locker that was ajar, and there it was. The note read: "Hey, baby, I just want you to know I'm always thinking about you. P.s. It's your baby, Vicky."

I thought I was in the clear, but if she didn't write this note that I had in my pocket, then who did? I thought to myself. "Thanks, baby. You know I'm always thinking about you, too," I replied with a kiss.

We all parted ways. Ceto took Nadine to class, and I walked Vicky to hers. Right before going to my class, I went to use the restroom to pee. I went to wash my hands after peeing and threw some water on my face, and no sooner had the water left my face than she was there—Joy was in the bathroom. "What the hell?"

Young Kaz

"Did I scare you, baby?" she said. She walked up to me, and she began reaching out and caressing my dick. I was shocked but enjoying the massage.

She backed me up against the wall and then pushed me into one of the toilets with a door on it. "I just want to taste you, Kaz," she said aggressively.

"Wait, don't do this," I said. I didn't want it to happen, but I couldn't fix my hands to stop her. I wanted it to, but before I could say anything else, it already happened. I was inside her mouth, and she started to suck. I continued to get harder.

"Oh, yes, Daddy. Get big for me," she moaned.

I knew that in seconds, it would be over, but I never thought that I would bust—or that quickly. I came in her mouth. While I was coming, she sucked every drop out of me and continued to suck as if I was a straw to get every drop. I was so drained that I stayed against the wall to rest, and she walked out like nothing had happened.

I went to class, barely walking straight, thinking, *What the fuck?* That girl had some soul-sucking lips. While letting my body rest in class, not even paying attention to what the teacher was saying, I drifted off, reminiscing about my mom's conversation:

"You have the ones that have no respect for themselves. They will sleep with every Tom, Dick, or Harry just to say they had them."

"That means they are sluts then, right?"

"Not really, baby. You see, those types of girls are like men. They think like men and act like men by trying to fuck everything that moves. When you see that type, run, boy." As the pictures played in my head, I could see Joy's sneaky smiles now.

The bell rang, and I popped up, realizing I had fallen asleep. I got my belongings and left. Before I knew it, school was out, and I was on my way home. When I reached home, I bumped into Marvin leaving.

"What's up, Pops? Where are you going?"

"To the store. What's up? You good?"

"Not really. I need to talk to someone," I said.

"Well, hop in. Let's go. So what's the issue?" he asked.

"There's this girl at school that has a thing for me. I know she knows I've got a girl, but she doesn't say a word. She walked right between me and Vicky today and spoke, but when she catches me alone, that's when she speaks."

"Sounds like she wants you to have your cake and eat hers, too," he said, smirking.

"What, Pops?"

"That's a good thing. She knows you have a girl but doesn't care. She's willing to keep it on the low. Some females do that shit all the time. They will have their man home and go out and cheat. That's why when you find that good one, you have to fall back from the rest. They will just cause problems for you."

"Too late," I hinted.

"It can't be that bad," he replied.

I looked at him before dropping the bomb on him. "This girl came into the bathroom, shoved me into the toilets where the doors were, and gave me the meanest head I've ever had." Marvin's eyes opened wider as the story got juicier. "Then I bust in her mouth."

"Hell yeah, that's my boy. You had condoms, right?"

"Nope, and yup, I bust in her mouth. She drained me." Marvin looked at me and became quiet. "What?" I said, nervous-looking.

"Man, you've got to be careful. Girls like that are dangerous. Did you see her swallow?" he asked curiously.

"No. After she finished, she got up and left."

"This might be bad, son. Girls like that can still get pregnant. They know tricks and shit."

"No way, Pops. I have to bust inside her—everyone knows that."

"My boy, you've got a lot to learn. There is this thing I call squash, squash! Girls will take your sperm from a condom or their mouth and put it inside a cooking baster, then shoot it inside themselves to get pregnant." My heart just dropped. "Yeah, man.

Sorry to tell you, but on the other hand, let's just hope this is not the case. Nest advice I can give you now is to just stay on the faithful path from this point," said Marvin.

"Yeah, you're right. That's the best advice for now," I agreed.

This was a small world we lived in. While driving with Marvin to wherever he was going, I saw Joy. "See, look, Pops. That's her right there," I pointed out. The sad part was that she was in another dude's face.

"Got damn, boy. That girl is a bundle of joy," he said.

"That's her name, too, Pops," I laughed.

"What, bundle?"

"Nah, Joy. Joy is her name," I told him before his phone rang.

"Hello? Yeah, baby. I saw him already. He's right here with me. Ok, love you too. That was your mom. She was worried about you."

We pulled up to this old vintage store, which looked like no one ever shopped there. "Hold tight. I'll be back."

Rickey Dudley

Not knowing how long Marvin would take to come out, I started turning the radio channel to find something good to jam to for a few minutes. I heard a little commotion coming from the other side of the store, so I got out to see what was going on, and Mick was smack dead in the center of it. He reached inside his pants, drew back, shot this kid in the head with no hesitation, and just turned and walked away, stone-cold style.

He had this cold, chill look to him. He showed no remorse, and it felt like a movie. He began walking away, and for some reason, he turned toward my direction, and we locked eyes with one another. I was scared and puzzled. I didn't know whether to say something or to keep my mouth shut. Really, I was thinking this dude was a fucking psycho. Then I felt Marvin grab me, throwing me into the car. "Whatever you do, don't tell your mother I brought you down here, ok?"

"I won't."

"Damn it, damn it, I didn't want you to see no shit like that. These boys nowadays don't have no fucking respect for nothing!" he yelled. I was curious to know why Mick shot him. He wasn't arguing with Mick; it was with someone else.

Marvin kept rambling about how young boys don't keep their cool and how he fucked up for even bringing me down here. I could see that it was bothering him, so I did my best to keep him calm. "It wasn't your fault, Pops. You didn't know this was going to happen. I understand a little bit about this cold world," I said, trying to comfort him. He gave me a look as if I was right, so I hoped that calmed him down a little bit. As we got closer to the house, he still looked a little bothered. I was straight. After all, I watched movies seeing people's heads blown off all the time, so it didn't bother me a bit.

That was just the first time I saw someone get killed in real life.

Young Kaz

We made it in the house, and I went straight to my room, and Marvin flopped onto the couch, watching T.V. I laid in my bed, just daydreaming about what a crazy day I'd just had. First, getting head in the bathroom and then witnessing a murder. The phone rang, and it was Vicky.

"Wow, finally. No 'peace, who's this'!" she first said.

"Hey, what's going on, beautiful?"

"Can you come over?" I froze. *What the fuck?* I thought. *Why does she want me to come over all of a sudden?* I was scared to go over there. After Mick looked at me, shit, I didn't know if he wanted to kill me because I witnessed him killing a guy.

"I just got in, baby. I'm tired," I tried to convince her.

"Please, baby?"

"Alright, give me a few," I said. "Hey, Pops. I'll be back," I told Marvin while heading out of the house.

"Ok, champ," he replied.

"Really, dude? You're not even going to ask me where I'm going?" I said to him, sounding worried.

"Hold on, mister. You ok? And by the way, where are you going?" he said jokingly.

"I'm going to Vicky's house. She wants to see me," I said.

"Ok, don't come home too late."

"If you walk four blocks up, right before you get to the school, that's her house. The green one," I volunteered, just in case.

"Are you sure you're ok?" he asked, looking concerned.

"Yeah, I'm good." I tried to sound confident but felt nervous as hell. I went into the kitchen to grab a knife, tucked it in my pants, and left, heading toward Vicky. So many thoughts were racing through my mind. I was wondering if Mick got her to get me out so he could kill me or if Vicky found out about me and Joy and would have her brother kill me.

Oh fuck, why was I even going to her house without the cops? I think my pride was getting in the way, me proving I wasn't scared by going over there. As I walked, it looked like I was doing a new dance with how my legs buckled. *Ok, Kaz! Here goes nothing.*

"Hey, Kaz. Come in."

"What? I thought you wanted me to pick you up?"

"Come in, scaredy cat. What's up?" I walked in, nervous as hell and looking around for signs of anyone else being home, like Mick. "Don't worry. No one is home yet, and I asked my mom. She's cool with you being over here." I went to sit on the couch to relax my nerves, thinking all types of shit, like why she didn't call me baby like every other time.

"Can I ask you a question?" she said.

"Sure, what's up?"

"Do you really love me?"

"To be honest, I don't even know what love is, but if love is this strange feeling that I feel for you and being happy with and around and willing to die to protect you, then yes, I do love you."

Vicky began kissing me and unbuckling my pants. I knew she was about to give me head. That's all I'd been getting from her every once in a while.

But this time, I couldn't let her do it. After knowing Joy's lips were down there, it felt wrong. Besides, being in her house, I definitely didn't want to get caught there. "Please, baby, not today. I'm not in the mood," I told her. I was exhausted mentally and physically.

"Ok, no problem." I could tell she was upset a little bit, but she crawled on top and started kissing me. I had to hold her up; the knife started to dig into my skin.

"Hold up, baby."

"Is there something wrong? I feel like you are pushing me away." I pulled the knife out of my pants and saw the look on her face.

"What the fuck is wrong with you?"

As soon as she said that, I heard keys inside the door. I stuffed the knife right back inside. As the door opened up, I noticed Mick was walking inside. He stopped, looked dead at me, and paused for a minute. "What's good, lil bro? Come with me to my room," he said.

"Give me a minute, baby!"

As I walked behind Mick, I told myself to stab him now, not to wait, because if I went inside that room, he might kill me. It was too late now as he held the door open for me to enter. I couldn't help myself. I did my best not to look at his statue, which I thought was in his mom's room. I stood in his room for about two minutes, uncomfortable, before he said a word. "I know you saw me kill that dude. I didn't want you to see that, but I had no choice."

"Can I ask you a question?"

"What you want to know, Kaz? Why did I kill him?"

"You could've pistol-whipped him or just beat him up?" I inquired.

"No, brother. Not in this game. I'm at a higher level in these streets."

"You mean like mob status?" I said.

"A little something like that, but not quite. It's not the life I condone."

"I don't understand. The room and you don't match?" I pointed out.

"This is how my room looked before I got caught up in the game. It's a reminder of my innocence as a little kid, and my dad had that statue. I know that's bugging you out, but if you look closely, you will see that it's a naked man that has broken handcuffs—a symbol of being free or escaping to be free," he said. I looked at the statue and saw the whole piece this time, and now I saw that it did have broken cuffs. Thank God. I thought this dude was a bit strange at first. "So just know, anytime you need me, I'm here for you no matter what!" he replied.

"And Ceto," I said, trying to save him.

"That's your people. Just make sure he stays in his lane. No disrespect, but I don't care about anybody else but my family and now yours."

I looked a little surprised and happy. For one, he didn't want to kill me, and two, knowing he was on my side made me feel at ease. "Hey, brother," he said, "when you get home, make sure you take that shit out of your pants. You might cut yourself." I gave him a look like, *how did you know?* He just winked at me and smiled. As soon as I opened the door, I saw Vicky's feet running back to the couch.

"What were you and my brother talking about? He never invites anyone into his room. You're the first."

"We just had a man-to-man talk, that's all. Some of it was about you." We chilled the rest of the day, talking about life and how unpredictable it can be at times. We watched some movies, a little bit of action and of course romantic movies, like "Lady and the

Tramp" as a nice finisher. It was about time for me to go home, so I gave Vicky a kiss and walked out of the house feeling like the man.

By the time I went to take my third step, I was scared shitless. I heard a loud ass horn that made me jump. "Kaz! Come on."

"Damn, Pops. You scared the shit out of me. What are you doing here anyway?"

"What am I doing here? No, buddy, your ass sounded scared, like you didn't even want to come over here. Shit, when was the last time you cared to tell me exactly where you were going? You pretty much cried for help."

"Yeah, you're right! I was scared as hell, but I'm cool now."

"Alright, good because you're going to have to deal with your mom." I didn't like the way he said that. It smelled like trouble on Mom's end. "Don't worry, she didn't seem too upset!"

"That's a good sign," I said.

We got to the house, and Mom was on the couch. She stopped me in my tracks from racing to my room. She said, "Kaz, I got a letter today from your school. It's saying that you have some lateness on here. The fact that you're doing good, I'm not going to get in your ass about it, but pick it up, okay, baby? Don't start messing up."

"I got you, Ma. I won't. Can I go, Ma? My phone is ringing." I was so anxious to get it.

"Yes, baby," she said. I raced to my room to grab the phone. It was Vicky—this girl couldn't get enough of me. I just left her house.

"Hello?"

"Just making sure my baby reached home."

"I'm not too far away from you. Of course, girl."

"Yeah, but you also have a knife on you. I don't know what's going on, and I know you're not going to tell me, but be safe, and don't do anything stupid."

"You know I'm not."

"Got to make sure you and my brother are cool now. He does dumb shit from time to time, and I don't want you to get caught up in his shit. Oh, and guess what? Nadine called me earlier and told me she was pregnant. I want a baby too now." The phone went silent for a few, and then I was relieved. "I'm just kidding, fool. You were breathing hard." She continued to laugh at me.

I figured now wasn't a good time to tell her about Joy. Maybe tomorrow when I walk her to class. Yeah, that sounded good. "Ok, baby, talk to you later."

"Alright, see you tomorrow. Good night, and love you."

I got in my room and opened my top dresser, and right there was a blunt already rolled. I forgot all about my baby. My thoughts were racing, but smoking this blunt was going to make it right. I lit my spliff and began puffing away all my problems.

Rickey Dudley

Y ou could say smoking weed gave me a tranquil type of high. I smoked the whole thing this time; normally, I'd take a couple of pulls and then put it out, but for some reason, I wanted to see what was on the other end. I think that's when you became a feen—just my opinion. I got so relaxed that I fell asleep fast. It was a peaceful nap at first, and then I began tossing, turning, and sweating like crazy.

I started seeing a blurry vision of someone walking toward me and calling my name. "Kaz, Kaz, you know who did this to me," said the strange voice.

I replied, "I don't know what you're talking about."

As the person got closer and closer, my blurry vision became clear. All I saw was some dude standing still with a hole in his forehead with blood racing down his face.

I bolted out of my sleep, drenched with sweat, only to see Pops on the side of the bed beside me. "You ok, baby boy? I'm here. It's just a nightmare. Relax and think of something positive. Go back to sleep. I'm right here." I did just that. I fell right back to sleep thinking about Vicky.

When I woke up, I almost stepped on Marvin. He was still lying on the floor, knockout, drooling, and snoring on one of my pillows on the floor. Mom came inside my room and asked me if I'd seen Marvin. When she heard the snoring, she looked down the side of the bed and started laughing. Marvin woke up hearing me and Mom teasing him.

"Oh man, that was the best sleep I ever had. You got to try it, babe," he said, sounding like a big kid.

"Yeah, ok. Come on, both of my babies, go wash up and get ready for breakfast."

"Where are my morning kisses, baby?" said Marvin.

"Not with that breath." Marvin went to give Mom a kiss, and she ran out of the room, yelling, "No yuck mouth!" They began running around the house like little kids. I got up to watch them. Mom was on one side of the couch with Marvin on the other; it looked like they were playing tag. These were the moments I captured mentally for memories. Mom looked so happy—I mean, I always saw her happy because we joked around a lot, but this time, really watching her and Marvin was like watching me and Vicky. Yeah, I would say they had that special kind of love.

Now, I know why the caged bird sings—because he's in love. Playing around ended as we began taking care of our hygiene and preparing for our day. After we all ate breakfast, they went to work, and I went to school. I realized I'd reached school early before my normal time. I had this weird feeling, but I just disregarded it. I went to my locker in the hallway and found another note. It said: "*I know what you taste like. Now I want to know what you feel like inside me."*

Young Kaz

I t's flattering but scary. "What's up?" asked Ceto.

"I found another note, bro. Here." As Ceto read the short note that was left, he didn't seem surprised. In a way, he was right about trashing it, but I still thought about Vicky catching one of these notes. How would I explain it?

"Yeah, bro, you have problems, but anyway, I have a problem at hand," he said.

"What's up?"

"I've been trying to contact my supplier for some time now. I just heard over the weekend that he got shot in the head." *And there goes that weird feeling again.* "I'm going to get whoever did that to my man. They've got to pay. I know you're going to hold me down, right?" Damen, Ceto was my brother, but he didn't know who he was really going up against.

"Damn, bro. Sorry to hear. You know I got you, but let the cops deal with that. You got a kid on the way to think about," I said, trying to get out of the retaliation.

"Yeah, maybe you're right." The thought of Ceto finding out that I know who did it bothered me. I didn't want him to feel like I double-crossed him by not telling him, but at the same time, there was a code to the streets. Telling him would make us become enemies because my girl's brother killed his friend, and if he killed my girl's brother, that would put us in a bad space. I didn't want that—I loved this girl; she was going to be my wife someday.

Me and Ceto parted ways, preparing for class and doing our work. Now I was at a standstill. Should I tell Vicky about Joy or keep my mouth shut? Wait, what the fuck was going on in here? I could see Vicky holding Joy.

"Vicky, what's up?" I whispered.

"I feel so bad, baby. She just found out that her brother got killed yesterday when coming back from the dean's office. Aww, baby, I feel so bad for her. She fell into my arms, and all I could do was just hold her, feeling real fucked up inside."

Vicky started crying, and I just held her. Everything just seemed too coincidental. With all that was happening, I needed a blunt to try to wrap my mind around this. This bundle of secrets that I had was killing me. Holding Vicky in my arms while she was crying brought me to shed a tear or two. I tried not to, being a man and all, but when I heard her cry, that was it.

I looked over at Joy as she looked at me with a little stare, noticing me holding Vicky as she continued to cry. All I could say was, "Sorry for your loss." After a while, me and Vicky parted ways from Joy. Separating my mind felt like quicksand; all this drama just pulled me under from nowhere and put me in depression mode.

"Thanks for coming to check on me, but I'm going to call you later, ok? Make sure you stay available. I have a surprise for you," Vicky said.

As I began to walk away, I heard a voice in the background. It was Joy calling me. I looked around to see if Vicky was close by, but it was like she disappeared into thin air. "What's up, Joy? Sorry again," I said.

"For what it's worth, I really didn't know y'all was talking like that, and she's mad cool, so don't worry, I'll back off. Oh, and just in case you feel like being a super boyfriend and being honest in telling her what we did, that wouldn't be a wise move on your part. No need to worry, ok? I won't say anything, either. Let's just forget what had happened."

"Yeah, I hear you, but I'm not that stupid to tell on myself. As far as your brother, I'm truly sorry for your loss."

"Thanks, I'm dealing with it, though. Anyway, take care."

Now I really feel bad, but something in my mind just switched as I watched her walk away. I thought about what it would be like to take her down. She seemed like she could keep her mouth shut. Well, I guessed I was in the clear now with these damn sticky notes, but I noticed another one sticking out as I came to my locker. I grabbed it, and it read: *Hey, sexy. Just saying I love you, and you really mean the world to me. See you later, love Vicky.*

Now that was cool, but I wondered if she was sending these side notes to test my loyalty. I put all my stuff in my locker because I didn't have any homework, so it didn't make sense to carry them home. Today was just another day bizarre day that went by quickly. I couldn't complain.

Rickey Dudley

I reached home, relaxing with a nice blunt to clear my mind, and then the phone rang. It was Vicky telling me not to smoke because she wanted me to be clear-headed for my surprise when I went over to her house later. It was too late for that. I had a blunt already burning while talking to her. Maybe by the time I went over to her house later, I'd be good. Better yet, let me clip this little joint out now. I wasn't even thinking about the surprise; I was just thinking about all the bullshit that was going on in my life right now.

I wanted to talk to Marvin about it, but a little part of me was saying to let me work this out myself—that was part of being a man.

I fell asleep for a few minutes and woke up at five after seven. Right when I opened my eyes, the phone rang. "Babe, you're still coming over, right?" asked Vicky.

"Yes, I'm getting dressed now and heading out."

"Ok, take a shower and put some smell goods on." I know what that meant. I did just that. I thought about what was in the theaters while preparing myself.

"Kaz, you hungry?"

"No, Ma. I'm about to go see Vicky."

"Ok, don't stay out too late." I started walking toward Vicky's house, guessing what this surprise could be, but it left me clueless. Before something could pop into my mind, I was already at her door, and it was opened before I could ring the bell.

"About time, bean head. Come in. I thought you were going to take forever. Did you eat yet?"

"No, I was about to, but I told Mom I was coming to see you."

"Good because I cooked you some food. I made mac and cheese, your favorite, fried chicken, with broccoli and cheese."

"Now that sounds good," I said.

"Now, I don't know if you drink or not, but I got some of my brother's Hennessy."

"What, you trying to get me killed, girl?"

"No, baby. We're going to enjoy ourselves."

Young Kaz

Vicky took my coat, threw it on the couch, and then went toward the kitchen. She looked at me and said, "Do you want dessert now or after dinner?"

Shit, if she was the dessert, I would have had that first, but I replied, "Food, and after it's digested, I'll have some dessert, but just a little bit. By the way, what is dessert?" I asked.

She said it was marinating. She was always bragging about her peach cobbler; well, I guessed today I would see just how good it was. She wasted no time; she lit some candles around the table where our plates were. She didn't pile the food up; it was a nice portion. Then she grabbed the remote and hit play. Right when I sat down, the song popped on by *Tony, Tony, and Tony* titled "Let's Chill." I can't lie, I felt special, and the mood was right. I wasted no time trying the food.

"Wow, girl, I didn't know you could throw down. These taste good," I said.

"Thanks, babe. Excuse me. I have to use the restroom." She smiled and looked at me as if she already knew her food was the bomb. She came over to me and kissed me and said she loved me before going to the restroom.

I continued eating, but I couldn't finish. I had a piece of chicken hanging from my mouth, but I couldn't bite into the chicken because I thought my eyes were playing tricks on me. I looked up to see Vicky standing butt-ass naked next to her bedroom door. My mouth dropped, along with the chicken. I swallowed what was left in my mouth, damn near making me choke, amazed by her body and looking at her from head to toe. Her hair was in a bun with the side baby hairs looking wavy with her beautiful eyes and lips.

Her breasts were sitting perky, she had no belly fat at all, her stomach was nice and flat, and her kitty was shaved. She had the Serena Williams thighs—nice and strong looking. She had pretty feet with no marks on her body at all. She must have known I was observing her body because she turned around for me to see her booty.

"Are you coming for dessert, or do you still want to wait?" I wasted no time. I got up and walked right toward her, kissing her and backing her up to her bed. I took my shirt off, then my tank top, and she started to unfasten my belt. She threw me on the bed and then hit the remote, playing the H-Town song, "Somebody Knocking The Boots." She licked me, starting from my chest down, putting all of me in her mouth, sucking away. I just fell back.

She sucked until I was rock hard, then laid on the bed and said, "I want you to be my first, but go easy." I was speechless. I didn't know what to say. I couldn't believe she was really a virgin and that this was about to happen. I crawled over her and asked, "Are you sure?"

She said, "Yes."

I told her I didn't have condoms, and she told me to go into her brother's room and get one. I got up as fast as I could, butt out and all.

Rickey Dudley

I walked into his room and looked right at the dresser, and there was a big bucket of condoms. I was a little nervous about being inside his room butt-ass naked. I backed up into that stupid ass statue, and it poked me in the butt. I ran out and back into Vicky's room to finish before she changed her mind.

"Slow down before you break something. We've got all night. Surprise!" I was really surprised. "I want to feel you first and then put the condom on."

Yeah, I wasn't expecting this. I got on top of her. I took my penis head and started rubbing her clitoris, hearing her moan. I did that for a few minutes, then inserted the head slowly. Her moaning started to get crazier. While I was inserting the head, the Maxwell song came on, titled "This Woman's Work." Now, both of them were moaning at the same time; Maxwell was moaning at the beginning of the intro, and so was Vicky. She grabbed me as I went inside her.

"It's all the way in, yeah?" she asked.

"No, that's only the head that's in," I said. "You want me to put more inside?"

She continued shivering and replied, "Yes!" I continued to put the rest inside as she moaned harder and scratched my back. I knew this was a night I would never forget. We started making love if that was what you called it. She was moaning while biting me. We were having sweaty, hot, passionate sex; she got on top and began riding me. She moved as slow as she could, taking the pain, and the more she rode, the louder her moans were and the harder I got. She was so tight, she made me come fast in a couple of strokes. "Hold up, I'm about to come." She got up off me just in time to see me come. I came so hard that some of it got on her breasts. "Sorry, baby."

"It's ok. It felt good," she said.

After I busted, she started jerking me off to make sure all of it came out. She went into the bathroom, came out with a rag, and swiped my penis off. Then she got right back on top and continued riding, but this time, she climaxed. She came so hard she lost her balance and fell all the way on my penis, shaking with me still inside her and moaning so hard that I got hard again. We just laid there with me inside her. Every now and then, she would move her pelvis a little, then just lay still on top of me. Man, I never got this hard. I wanted more. I started humping just a little bit, letting her know I was ready to go again.

"Baby, please let me rest now." I was ok with that. After all, that took a lot out of me. We lay there for a few minutes, then after she got up, she went into the shower, and I took the rag and wiped myself some more. I went to get some food.

"Can you make me a plate, babe?"

I tell you, I felt like I was on top of the world. I made her plate and mine and waited for her to come out so we could eat together.

Young Kaz

fter she came out of the bathroom, she gave me a sweet, innocent look. "Are you ok?" I asked.

"Yes, I was bleeding. Is that supposed to happen?"

"Yes, it's called popping your cherry." I started joking, saying that I had popped her cherry, but she looked like she wasn't in the mood to laugh.

"That's not funny," she said. She put her head down as if she was sad.

"Are you sure you're ok? I didn't mean to hurt you. If I did, I'm sorry!" I said sincerely.

After my response, she held her head up and said, "No, baby, you didn't hurt me, but my kitty is hurting. It's a good pain, though."

We ate and talked while listening to some nice soft music for a while. I looked into her eyes awkwardly, knowing that I wanted to be in her life forever. Today was the day I made love to my wife; that was a mental note.

Part of me wondered what was going on in her mind. The day was ending with me at Vicky's, and now I was on my way home to prepare for bed and school.

Just before hitting the corner to my house, I noticed the cops were leaving, so I walked a little faster with my mind racing, but as I reached the door, Marvin spotted me and held the door open.

"Pops, what's up? What's going on?" I asked.

"They just dropped me off. They had me down there for questioning, asking about that murder that happened near the store the other day. They had me on camera, and yes, they got you too, so it's only a matter of time before they come back and want to question you as well."

"Aww, man. I didn't do it," I said, sounding scared.

"No need to worry. I'll be there with you. Just tell them what you saw, which was nothing, and you will be ok," he said.

I'd never had any run-ins with the cops; I wouldn't know what to do or say, so I did what any scared kid would do: I told the truth with a little bit of a lie. I told Marvin what happened so he could coach me through it.

"Pops, I saw the killer, but I don't want to be labeled a snitch."

"Do you realize what you're saying? Someone's son got killed. If it was my son, I would want the killer turned in," he said.

"I understand, but what if you were in my position, where you saw the person get killed that you didn't know, but you think you may know who the killer is, then you go to school to find out that the girl that gave you head in the bathroom is now crying on the girl's family member that's responsible but doesn't know it yet. And with a best friend that wants revenge for that same murder, and the worse part is, before the murder happened, the person that did the killing swore to protect you."

"Ok, so clearly you know who it is, but I also understand that's a tough situation, and to answer that, yeah, I'd probably keep my mouth shut if I was in your shoes. Don't worry, your secrets are safe with me. I thought I had problems, but damn, kid. Seems like you got a little more going on in your life than I do."

"Yeah, sometimes bad and sometimes good," I said. I put a smile on my face that said, *I just got some pussy.*

"Alright, now spill the beans. I know that smile from anywhere. Talk to me," said Marvin.

Rickey Dudley

We started walking straight to my room so I could give him the juicy details of me tearing Vicky's back out, but I heard Mom's voice before we could reach my room. "What the hell! No one sees me over here? Hello!"

"Sorry, Mom!" I replied, kissing her to keep her calm, and so did Marvin. You could say she got a double kiss. Marvin kissed one side and me the other, and we mushed her face with kisses to the point her lips were popping out, looking like a blowfish. We went to my room to finish our conversation.

"Where was I, Pops? Oh yeah, so I went to Vicky's house because she had a surprise for me. I got fresh, you know how I do! I put some cologne on because I thought she was taking me out, but when I reached her house, she cooked some food for me. She made some bomb-ass mac and cheese, fried chicken, and broccoli and cheese. She asked me if I wanted dessert now or later, and I said later because I thought it was a peach cobbler, but the kitty cat was the dessert. Anyway, right after I ate a few bites, she was sitting butt-ass naked for me in front of her room. So, you know I took it down. I had that girl crying out my name."

As I gossiped to Marvin, all you could hear was, "What? Yeah, that's my boy!"

He told me that was good but to stay away from the rough ride. I never figured out why they called it a rough ride, but it was too late for that. Then I dropped the other bomb, telling him I was her first, and his mouth dropped to the floor. "Now that's major champ good shit, but one thing—being that you are her first, you have to be careful not to break her heart."

"Yeah, I know!" I told him. Marvin and I finished our conversation, he left the room, and I went straight to bed. I didn't even shower; I kept her sweet virgin smell on me. I laid back in bed, and that was it, off in a dream world. I had a dream about Vicky. I was inside her, making love, but only this time, I came like a volcano. She was still on top of me, and my sperm shot inside her like water, and her belly grew without stopping.

She grew so big that she burst, causing me to wake up out of my dream in a puddle of sperm. Now that was a good dream. I woke up on demand just in time to shower and leave for school.

I almost forgot to get my books out of my locker when I arrived. Before going to class, I went to my locker and saw there was a note sticking out. I grabbed the note to read it.

Joy punched me on the arm out of nowhere. "See you later, Kaz," she said.

I looked at the letter and then her again. I shouted out, "Yo, what's up with this?" referring to the note. Just before she turned the corner, she yelled, "That wasn't me." I was in a daze, thinking it had to be Vicky.

Young Kaz

I opened the note to see a small drawing of a pair of lips, and it read: "*Meet me in the gym locker room around lunchtime, and don't take long.*" I thought about Ms. Rodriguez, but I doubted it was her. She wouldn't want anyone to know because she would get in trouble.

I grabbed my books and proceeded to my class, wondering who it could be. For most of the lesson, I drifted away thinking about the note; I had no clue. As time passed by, my mind went back to Vicky. What a night that was. I would never forget it.

Before I could finish thinking about my baby Vicky, the fire alarm went off. The teachers gathered all the students and instructed us to go outside. When everyone was finally out, Mr. Hill got on the bullhorn. "Ok, everyone, listen up. Give us a few to see what's going on, and we'll have y'all back inside in no time."

We really didn't care because no one wanted to do classwork. I stood in one spot, letting my mind just roam, and then I felt someone covering my eyes from behind. "Guess who?" It was Vicky. I knew that beautiful voice from anywhere. "You got my note, right?"

I gave her a look, but the look was a satisfying one, knowing now who sent the note. "Yeah, I got it."

She kissed me, said, "Ok, don't be late," and returned to her friends.

"Ok, everybody, back inside. The school is still open," said Mr. Hill. Everyone went inside. With only three minutes left, the teacher decided to end the class early. I sat daydreaming for a minute or two, and the bell rang.

I went to the locker room to see Vicky, and the moment I stepped inside, I was pushed against the wall. "What are you doing in here, Mr. Kaz?" said Vicky.

I caught on quickly. "Well, I was told to meet someone in here." "You not dealing no drugs, are you, son?"

"Hell yeah, I even got some for you!" We both began to laugh at this good-girl-bad-boy theme.

"Vicky, why are we in here? You know you can get in trouble, right?" I reminded her.

"It's lunchtime. Besides, no one is coming in here. Let me pull it out." I looked at her, surprised, but I didn't stop her. She began to rub my private area as if it were hers.

"Excuse me, miss. What are you doing here?" I asked playfully.

"I couldn't sleep last night. I felt you inside me and couldn't wait to see you. Let me just suck you a little bit, baby," she said. She pulled it out and began sucking. I was enjoying the moment until I heard a loud bang. "Hold on, I think someone's coming," I told her, but she didn't even budge. She was going to town on me like she would never see me again. Now there were footsteps. "I know you heard that," I whisper to her, but still she didn't listen.

"310 to base all clear," said the stranger. Now I know she heard that because she paused while I was still inside her mouth.

She mumbled, "I heard that!" Thinking that the coast was clear and hearing the person say it was, I guess Vicky thought the person had left, so she kept going.

"What the fuck are y'all little nasty asses doing in here?" yelled Ms. Williams.

Rickey Dudley

y heart dropped into my ass, and so fast, I went from Hard Rock Daddy to Mr. Softy in seconds. I wasn't the only one who felt fucked up. Vicky jumped a little bit, scraping her teeth on my penis. Right after, she paused, as if no one could see her, and I wanted to laugh so bad because Vicky was still on her knees with my dick inside her mouth like no one could see her. In the future, I knew I would be crying about this moment, but not right now. I was scared as hell.

"Girl, if you don't get your silly ass up off your knees. Take your ass to class," Ms. Williams shouted. There was something strange about Vicky. She never sucked me that good. *I got it—her ass is high as hell*, I thought, watching her get off her knees.

She bounced off her knees and took flight in mid-air, like how the cartoon character would run. Looking at Ms. Williams, I was soft and frozen in one spot. I was trying stealth mode like a deer caught in headlights.

She looked at me and said, "Now I wonder what the hell she was doing?" referring to my little softy. "Your little ass shouldn't be here anyway." I noticed a little smirk as she finished her sentence while looking down at Mr. Softy. I felt a little bad, but something crazy started happening. I looked at her breast and thought about sucking them, and my Mr. Softy started to transform into Mr. Big Daddy. "Oh no, not now…" I whispered to myself, but I saw her facial expression while she watched me get harder, and her face went from a smirk into an *oh ok* expression.

I felt a little draught from the little bit of moisture that Vicky had left, which made me go rock hard in no time. I looked at her face once more, and she looked back at me. I looked down and then back at her as if I didn't mean to get hard and smiled.

"Put that thing away!" she said. The weird part was the little conversation about her reprimanding me, and she wasn't looking in my eyes. "Now go to class, and don't let it happen again, you nasty fucker," she said. "If anyone sees us leaving here, I will have to report y'all, understand?"

I understood exactly what that meant—that was a close call. I left as fast as I could while fixing my pants. When I reached the lunchroom, I saw Vicky sitting, eating like nothing happened.

I sat at the table, and she just looked at me and then licked her lips. "You taste good, Daddy," she whispered. I didn't know what had gotten into her, but I liked this freaky side, just not in public. "I'm sorry, baby, I had some weed earlier with a shot of patron." That explained it all. Shit, I knew to bring that combination next time so we could have a ball—duly noted.

"Baby, I love you," she said.

"Love you too," I replied.

As the day was coming to an end, I heard the ice cube voice. "Today was a good day!" While walking Vicky home, we spoke about our future. "I really love you and don't want to be with anyone else. I hope you feel the same way," said Vicky.

Young Kaz

"Of course I do, but we can't predict the future at all. What we can do is just see what happens."

I gave Vicky a kiss, and then I began to walk home.

Truthfully, I couldn't see myself being with anyone else. I felt like the happiest man on Earth.

When I arrived home, no one was there. I went to make some food when the phone rang, so I picked up the phone in the kitchen. That was when I noticed a little blood on the floor. Before picking up this phone, I paused, saying, "Please, God, don't let this be bad news." I was thinking the worst. "Hello?"

"Hello, baby."

"Mom, what's up?" I said with a sigh of relief. "What's going on?"

"I'm in the hospital with Marvin. Don't worry, he's ok. The doctor said he had high blood pressure. His nose was bleeding like crazy. Anyway, I just wanted to let you know where we were, and don't worry about the blood. I'll clean it when I get back. Ok, love you."

As I got off the phone, I noticed a blood trail going from the kitchen to the bathroom. Damn, he'd lost a lot of blood. It was a good thing Mom told me before I saw all this or I would've gone into shock.

I made some cereal and sat in the living room to watch TV. I sat just in time to watch the new series of Power. Now it was my phone going off, so I sat my bowl down and went to answer it. Not many people called me, just Vicky or Ceto—speaking of, I didn't see him in school today.

"Primo, what's up?" Ceto asked.

"Don't 'what's up' me, bro. Why didn't you come to school?"

"I wasn't feeling good, bro. I think I got the flu or some shit."

"Damn, bro. Well don't bring your ass to school until you get better. I don't want to catch that shit."

Part of me wanted to tell him about me and Vicky's episode, but that would be disrespectful on her part, so I kept it shut.

"I'll be back at school tomorrow. I got a surprise for you," said Ceto. Last time he said that he brought me some weed. I couldn't even gather my thoughts about what this surprise could be.

"Ok, see you tomorrow."

I hung the phone up and went right back to eating my cereal. I turned the channel over to music videos, forgetting all about the new series I was starting, and before I could get comfortable, there was a knock at the door. I didn't want to answer it because I was scared it might be the cops. I was nervous as hell, so I turned the TV down a little bit and ignored the knock. The knocking had stopped, and my belly was nice and full. I set the bowl on the table and went right to sleep.

When I woke up, it was 6:30 A.M. The bowl was in the kitchen, the blood was off the floor, and Mom's room door was closed—what?! She left me on the couch.

I did my daily hygiene norm and put some music on while I got ready for school. I slept well, ate well, and got my smell-goods on. I was ready to start my day.

Rickey Dudley

Just before leaving, I gave Mom a kiss and said later to her and Pops. Before I touched the doorknob, Marvin said, "School is coming to an end, so start planning now for your future." I started thinking while walking to school about what college I was going to go to and what it would be like to go there.

Then I got interrupted by Ceto. "Yo, hold up." He caught up, and I noticed he was holding his pelvis and running weirdly. "Bro, let's go straight to the bathroom," he said, almost out of breath. We did just that, and when we got inside, we said what's up to everyone we knew and went straight there.

"Look at this shit, bro," he said. He pulled out a nine-millimeter black and chrome. I must admit, it had my attention.

"This is nice. I got to get me one," I said, showing that I was down for the cause but not really serious about getting one.

"Don't worry. I already got yours in the works. My partner is looking out for me. Shit is getting real out here, bro. We got a block to hold down now," said Ceto.

When he said that, I knew trouble wasn't far around the corner, but being a good friend and damn near brother, I had to do my part. I told him, "Come on, bro. You are better than that. You know what that leads to. You got a kid on the way, bro."

"Yeah, I know, but Nadine's mom made her get an abortion, and I already got in the groove of holding the block down, so it's too late getting out now. You down with me, right?"

Now, I was no punk, but that was a hard pill to swallow. I wasn't about that life. The only thing I knew was how to eat, sleep, shit, and get laid. But like a true homey that was down for the cause, I said yes anyway. "Of course, bro. I got your back."

We went to class, but for some reason, the class looked strange today. We had a substitute teacher who didn't have a clue about what he was doing. The principal made a change for today, and he moved our class around, taking kids out and placing them inside other classes with different teachers. The cool part was that me, Ceto, Vicky, and Nadine wound up in the same room. We were all having the times of our lives as we didn't have any work to do, so we were having fun—rolling up paper, throwing it at one another, spitballs, and everything.

Once the teacher came inside, we stopped. "Listen up. Today we have a special class. We have visitors from other classes, but sorry, guys, your teacher left work for y'all." Just before the teacher began to speak, he looked at the door, which caused everyone to look. It was the police.

"My name is Officer Baker, and this is Officer Thomas. We would like to speak with Kaz Johnson."

I sat still. The cops didn't know who I was, but the class and the teacher gave me away. You could hear the "Ooh, someone's in trouble."

The teacher said, "Kaz! Go with these officers."

Young Kaz

The whole class turned, looking in my direction. "Kaz, what's going on?" Ceto whispered.

"I have no clue, bro," I whispered back.

"Let's go. We don't have all day," said Officer Baker.

I walked down the steps feeling like I was walking into hell. I walked into the hallway with the cop. "We want to talk to you about the murder of Alex Jefferson," said Officer Thomas. While he said Jefferson, Joy walked by, going into the same classroom I just came out of.

"What the hell were you doing over there by Cypress Hills?" Officer Baker shouted.

"I was over there with my Step Pops," I answered.

"For what?" Officer Baker yelled.

"I don't know. I just got out of school, went home, and noticed he was heading somewhere. I just wanted to go with him because I wanted to talk to him," I said nervously.

"About what the murder of Alex?" Officer Baker shouted.

"No!" I replied, scared. "I didn't kill anyone."

He seemed to be accusing me of murdering Alex Jefferson. I noticed his posture was becoming aggressive, as if he was seeking revenge for Alex, who may have been someone he knew.

His partner held him back, saying, "Listen, if you didn't do it, that's good, but if you know something about it, you need to come clean. We will be in touch," said Office Thomas. They walked away and left me standing by the door in tears and breathing heavily.

I looked at the door, trying to decide what to do; should I go back to class or just go home? I made the decision to go inside. Besides, I had my stuff in here. I walked straight to my seat with my head down.

"What's up, kid? What's going on?"

"I have no clue, bro. They were asking me about some shit I have no clue about."

"Ok, listen up. Let me do my attendance sheet. When you hear your name, say 'here.'" He called each name, and the next name was when all hell broke loose. "Joy Jefferson?"

When he said Jefferson, I looked up at her only to see her staring at me. The look she gave me was a cold look, a look that could kill. I put my head down, feeling so twisted inside, wishing this day would end. I held my head down, pretending I had a massive headache, but it wasn't fooling anyone. Everyone knew I was embarrassed or stressed about being in trouble with the law, but holding my head down gave me a little piece of tranquility.

"Ms. Jefferson, please sit back in your seat," the teacher asked about five times, making me lift my head to see what was happening. I lifted my head and saw Joy standing before me with tears racing down her face. Before I could say a word, Joy swung at me, gunning for my face. I threw my hand up to block it, but I watched as Vicky dove at her, beating her ass before I could get up.

Rickey Dudley

I went to break it up, telling Ceto to grab Joy as I grabbed Vicky. The teacher called for security, and they were there in no time to escort us to the dean's office. In the process, Joy was yelling from the top of her lungs at me.

"You motherfucker. You had something to do with my brother's death. I swear to God, I'm going to kill your ass." Vicky and Ceto paused and looked at me in shock. I was speechless.

I didn't know what to say. All I could say was, "I didn't kill your brother!" Ceto gave me a look as if I'd backstabbed him, and Vicky was disgusted with me; she wouldn't even hear me out. I felt alone and cast out all in one day. I decided to stay in the dean's office and wait until either my mom or Marvin came to pick me up. "Mr. Jordan, please go with the nurse."

I heard the nurse approach me. "Come, let's get some stitches for that," she replied.

I said, "Stitches for what?" while attempting to wipe my hand of a sting I felt. Now that my nerves had calmed, I noticed I had an open wound on my hand. Oh, the bitch had cut me. That would've been my face if I didn't block it.

As I went with the nurse, I saw Ceto holding Joy in his arms as parts of the story unfolded. Ceto's homeboy turned out to be Joy's brother. Ceto knew a little about his boy's killing, and Joy thought I did it or had something to do with it. Vicky felt I'd deceived her by not saying anything about it. This was one of those days where I just wanted to move and get away from all the shit that was happening. I felt like the Atlas statue; life was getting heavier. My hand got sewed up in time, and my mom and pops were waiting in the principal's office.

Mom came out of the office when I got there, not even saying a word. "Let's get the hell out of here," Marvin replied.

We walked out of school, heading to the car. I looked over to see Joy in cuffs. I guess the cops found the blade she had on her. She was still giving me this cold look. From that stare, I learned what being targeted as a dead man felt like. As we drove away, the classroom watched from the windows, as if there was more to come.

There were only two weeks left of school before it was over. Based on the circumstances, I had to sign an agreement not to come back to school, but the principal was cool. He said, "Being that your grades are outstanding, you were going to complete high school anyway." He gave me two weeks off early. He also said, "Don't worry. Your diploma will be mailed to you, but once again, based on what has happened, I can't afford for you to come to prom or walk the stage."

I thought it was cruel, but then again, it was a good thing; the embarrassment I would've had to face, or better yet, the ridicule from others, would've been unbearable.

By tomorrow, it was going to be all over the school. I was ok with the agreement, so I was officially out of school and didn't know what to do with myself.

Young Kaz

On the ride home, I noticed it was quiet. I finally found one bad reason why living close to the school was a bad idea: making it home too quickly when you were in trouble.

I wasted no time; I closed my eyes and began to pray silently. *"Father, God, please help me. I'm in a time of need. I didn't do anything. Please touch my mom and help her to understand. Amen. Oh, and God? Give me the strength to run, just in case you can't get through to Mom. Amen."*

We pulled up to the house, and Mom got out with Marvin. I waited because I was no fool. "Kaz, what's up? Let's go. What are you waiting on?"

Shit, a sign from the Lord, I said to myself. "No disrespect, Pops, but I'm not getting out of this car unless the cops are here with me."

"Thought you feared the cops?" he asked.

"Nope, not at all."

"I'm lost here, man. What's up?"

"I'm terrified of Mom. Man, you don't know her. Let's just say I'd rather get hit by Mike Tyson than get hit by her."

Marvin just laughed as if I was telling a joke, but I gave him that look like, *Ok, you think I'm joking? I was dead as serious.*

"Nah, you're good, man. I spoke with your mom and explained all the details, except about you knowing who killed the kid. I see now why you didn't want to say anything, and you were right, it's a lot to deal with. Come on. Let's get some grub."

I got out of the vehicle, walked right behind Marvin, and went straight to my room. "Kaz, come back in here," Mom shouted. I heard the tone of my mom's voice; it didn't sound like she was upset, but I was still cautious.

"Yes, Ma!" I said sweetly to remind her I was her baby and only child.

"Why didn't you tell me what was happening? I would have listened to you."

"Well, Ma, I thought by me being grown, I could handle my own problems for once, but I guess I didn't do a good job at it."

"Marvin told me everything, and from the looks of it, you did the best you could. That was a tough situation to be in. You've had enough stress for the day. We'll talk about this another time— better yet, when you're ready, ok? Go get some rest, baby," she said.

"Ok, Ma. Thanks for understanding," I told her.

I went inside my room, grabbed what little I had left of my weed, and rolled up some nice ones. I was able to roll up a good three good joints. Afterward, I reached back to put my music on, thinking about Vicky, and then the phone rang. My baby must have missed me, too.

I raced to pick the phone up. "Hello?" But on the other end, I heard a not-so-familiar voice.

"Hello, I have your order ready, Mr. Max. Can you send us your information so we can mail it to you?"

"Max doesn't live here," I said and hung up the phone.

My days had become normal: take a couple of pulls, just enough to feel nice, and make it last by clipping it out. I clipped my joint short because I wouldn't be able to get any more from Ceto. I would party in my room by myself, come out every now and then to eat, shit, and see what Mom and Pops were up to, then go back to my room.

Rickey Dudley

I did this until the weed was gone, almost making it to a week. With only two days out before everyone could enjoy the day that meant the most to them, which was prom night, my stomach was in knots.

I wondered who Vicky was with, if she was even thinking about me, and then I thought about my brother, Ceto. Shit, it was times like this I knew I could count on him for entertainment, but that time had passed. All I had now was my mom and pops in my corner.

"What's good, man? You not going out anywhere?" asked Marvin.

"I would, Pops, but there's nowhere to go. Ceto won't speak to me because that was his boy who got killed, and Vicky feels like I lied to her. All I've got is you and Mom. I don't have anybody else."

"Don't worry. I'm telling you, all this will pass. Have you even tried to call Vicky? I doubt she'd call it quits that fast."

"What makes you so sure about that?" I asked.

"Let's see. First, you took her virginity, and second, y'all in love. Yeah, she's not going nowhere anytime soon, champ. Give her a call," Marvin insisted.

"That's right, baby. Give her a call," Mom cheerleaded in the background.

They gave me a little courage. "I guess y'all right, but what if—"

"Just give the girl a call, man," said Marvin.

I sat by the phone, trying to figure out what I would say to her, wondering if she would even pick the phone up at all. *Here goes nothing.*

The phone kept ringing. No one picked the phone up. After about a good minute of trying to get through to her, I just hung the phone up and gave up.

I walked out to the living room. "Sorry, guy. No answer. I think she's done, but it's ok. Like you said, I'll get over it."

Like a sad puppy, I walked back to my room and flopped onto my bed. I felt so hurt and lonely; I didn't want to cry, but for some reason, one tear fell. I heard a beep, which was the alert that the radio was about to come on. The song by Lewis Capaldi, "Someone You Loved," was on. That song brought everything out of me, and I cried like a baby. It was like that song possessed me. I got up and blasted that damn song. It all but emptied my tears from me. "Damn you, Lewis."

Marvin popped into the room; he'd never done that before. "Hell yeah, that's that shit right there, Kaz," he yelled. I couldn't help but realize he had tears streaming down his face, too.

I was the hurt one in a sad mood, so I gave him a stare like, *Dude, seriously?* Mom came rushing in, laughing. "You big ass babies. What grown man cries?" she said.

"A real man!" Marvin replied. "Real men are not scared to cry. Y'all forget we have emotions and are humans, too." After his reply, he went back into lip-syncing, the song falling out of him, being all dramatic.

Young Kaz

Mom was watching us act out. "Let's go out, Kaz. Get ready. I'm going to take you out, just us men. No little girls."

I gave him a look like, *Really, dude?* I reminded him about the last time I went out with him. I'd been in the house for some time now, so a little excitement would be good. "Ok, Pops. Y'all can get out of my room now and let me freshen up," I said.

They carried on like love birds, flying out of my room. I had to clear my mind or else I would go crazy crying over Vicky. I pop one of my CDs in the stereo, the song "You Don't Have To Call" by Usher. That song always put me in playboy mode. I got fresh and threw some cologne on as a finishing touch, ready to tour the world. I felt reborn again.

"First stop is Target."

"Wait, Pops, I thought we were going out to hang out? You know, men stuff!" I said, sounding confused.

"Yeah, that's what we're doing."

"At Target, Pops, really?"

"That's right, baby boy. We are hanging."

I just got punked. I wanted to experience something new to clear my mind, and this is what he came up with. I want to get turned out! Wait, that didn't sound right. Let me just relax myself. Besides, I'd run out of snacks, so this was a good time to load up.

On our way to Target, we passed by my old school. A little memory went through my mind of when I first started—the good, the bad, and the ugly. We drove for about a half hour before reaching our destination.

"Ok, champ. We're here—look alive," Marvin said, alerting me that the time had come. I guessed this was what old people got into as they aged.

While he was parking, I looked to my right just before opening the door, and I noticed this fine girl talking to a lady who appeared to be her mom, I assumed. I cracked the door ajar just enough to hear her voice and waited for her to get in her car so I could get out of mine. That's when it happened; she gave me the stare-down, which felt like forever.

"Oh, I'm sorry. I didn't see you there."

In the background, I heard Marvin whispering, "Go ahead, champ. Work it!" I got gassed up. I got out of the car, ready to engage in conversation, but shorty just closed the door, and they drove away. I turned to see if Marvin was ready, and he was laughing his ass off.

I admit, it was kind of funny. I saw that the day was just starting, and I felt good already. I felt alive again. Marvin and I walked into Target with a pimp stroll. We started getting carried away, bugging out, and having fun. It felt like we were on a mission. Marvin would see something and point it out to me, saying, "Alright, let's see what you got," signaling for me to go and catch it. So you know me, I did my one-twos, showing him I wasn't scared. I bagged girls for a living, but it wasn't working today for some reason.

Rickey Dudley

At this point, I didn't care. I was having fun just approaching them. From the looks of it, Marvin was having fun sending me off and watching me get shut down. I got shut down so many times, and I enjoyed it.

What the hell, why not raise the levels? I started going after grown women now. With all the practice and getting shut down, I gained more confidence in approaching women. Conjuring up a conversation became easy for me, and that's when I saw her. Short, around five-six or five-seven in height, with long hair that came down past her shoulders, a small waistline, a body only God could create, and a caramel complexion with green eyes. I was stuck. I just stared at her how I imagined a lion would stare at a gazelle when it was dinner time.

"Are you ok, honey? You look like you just saw a ghost," she said.

"Yeah, a beautiful one at that. Almost looked just like you!"

"Oh, I'm flattered. Thanks, young man," she said, blushing.

"You're welcome, beautiful, and I'm not that young. I'm 20 years old."

"Yes, baby, you're young. I'm pushing mid-30s, so to me, you're young." I was so tired of getting played out. I had nothing to lose, and there was no way I was getting her. I just vented and let it all out. What's the worst that could happen? She would either walk away or just say no. I wouldn't be disappointed; besides, this wouldn't be the first.

I said, "I know I'm young, miss, but no disrespect, I'm hanging down there, and it gets hard as hell. I'm quite sure I can make you throw the towel in, but we will never know, right? Because your response may be, 'Oh, boy, please, you can't handle this,' or 'I don't rock the cradle,' right? My question to you would be, how would you know if you don't give this cradle a chance? You never know. This cradle just may rock you."

"Yes, you're right. You are too young for me, and I don't rock the cradle, but I like how you come off strong, and you're handsome, too. I'll tell you what, take this first. Here's my number, and we'll see. Maybe I'll just give you a chance. Today is your lucky day, young man."

How she looked at me when I spoke caught me off guard. She started smiling like I was a cute little puppy, and most of all, I was surprised by her giving me her number.

"Word, I mean, are you just going to write your number down and walk off? Who am I supposed to ask for, that sexy ghost from Target?" I replied.

"Oh, boy, you too much. Step one, my name is Lisa. What's yours?" My name is Kaz, but you can call me whatever you want."

"Ok, Kaz. See you later."

As she turned away, I thought to myself, *What the hell? Her body is just amazing.* Before I could snap out of watching her walk away, I heard a creepy laugh—you know, that type of laugh when you're trying to hold it in but can't, so it just bursts out?

Young Kaz

"Come on, son. That's too much for you, but I don't blame you for trying."

"You right, Pops. Question, though... Should I call her now or later?" I showed off the number.

His mouth dropped, and I just gave him a smirk. I felt like I had accomplished a lot today. I got rejected so many times that I got upset and careless, but all those times I got turned down weren't equal to this one number I got. She looked better than all the other girls I tried to holla at. As I got into the car, my mind started to roam around, and for some strange reason, it went back to the dude getting shot, the images flashing right before my eyes, but this time, I was getting hot flashes of seeing the dude falling to the ground.

We got back to the house, and I gave Mom a kiss and went straight to my room to kick back. Before I could close my eyes, I heard, "Oh hell no, champ. You got to spill the beans and tell me the story," Marvin insisted.

"What story?" I acted as if I was clueless about what Marvin was talking about.

"You know, with the home girl at the store. Stop playing."

"Oh, no sweat," I replied, feeling like the man. I broke everything down in detail as far as me being turned down so many times that I just didn't care anymore. I decided to be an asshole mixed with cocky swag.

"Oh yeah, get ready, champ, because she's going to try that ass. You better be ready, and whatever you do, just let me know before you go to see her so I can give you some pointers."

"I got this, Pops!"

"Nah, son, you don't understand. When that day comes, it's like a championship fight. You've got to train like hell and have a coach in your corner. Trust me, I know what I'm talking about."

There was never a doubt in my head that Marvin didn't know what he was talking about, but I wanted to know—what was the fight about? And why is it so important to let him know when I get ready to see her? I'd wait until the day to see, I guess.

"Ok, champ. Get your rest. You're going to need it," he said as if I'd started training.

My eyes shut as soon as he cut the light out and closed the door. I fell into a deep sleep, and it felt so good. My body felt like it was healing itself. Suddenly, the phone rang. I was so weak, but I managed to reach out and grab the handle.

"Hello?"

"You know who did it and didn't help me."

Right as I tried to reply, I heard a gunshot go off, and I bounced up. My reaction wasn't to hang the phone up because it wasn't in my hand. Not knowing what to think of that dream, I tried to close my eyes and go back to sleep quickly. Before I could go back into that deep sleep, I felt something that seemed to be raindrops hitting my face, but it was rhythmic; a three-second count, and then the drop happened, and it was continuous.

Rickey Dudley

I reached to wipe my face, but before touching my face, I felt something that made me open my eyes. I was scared as shit; the dude that got shot by Mickey was hovering right over my face. His eyeballs were big, and I couldn't catch my breath. When I tried to exhale, he just screamed in my face while his head exploded.

I bounced up out of my bed and hit my head on the dresser. That was one hell of a dream. I couldn't go back to sleep after that, so I kicked back, put the TV on, and just watched the news. What do you know, who was on? Mick. Not Mickey Mouse, but Mickey, Vicky's brother. I guessed someone had turned him in. For some reason, I found great relief in him being turned in, knowing I didn't snitch on him. No one wanted to have the reputation of being called a rat.

I must have laid on my bed for a while, not even looking at the news, just listening to it. I admired the pictures on the wall, and of course, I saw that one picture that brought back good memories of Vicky. I wondered how she was doing. I wanted to call her so bad. I missed her.

It was around five o'clock in the morning, and I was just lying in my bed, no weed or anything. I reached out to grab 50 Laws of Power, written by Robert Greene and 50 Cent. I read until I got tired, which was a total of 30 minutes. I closed my eyes, only to open them to see 50 Cent staring at me.

"Oh, shit, it's you!" I said.

"You going to get out of my seat, punk, or do I have to move you?" 50 replied.

I yelled again, "It's really you!"

I looked up only to see his security storming inside the office, rushing toward me. They picked me up quickly and threw me out of the building. While flying out of the building, I thought to myself, *This must be how Jazz feels on "The Fresh Prince of Bell Air" when Uncle Phil throws him out of the mansion.*

I woke up laughing my ass off. "Kaz, come and eat, baby," Mom shouted. Damn, what time was it? It was only two in the afternoon—another day out of school, and I had no clue what I wanted to do with my life.

The phone rang, and it was Marvin. "Kaz, do you want to go with me to Target, but we are going food shopping this time? Mom needs something from there. If you don't, it's cool."

"Yeah, Pops," I said, knowing nothing else was happening for me right now. "Let me eat first."

"Yeah, no worries. I'm on my way to the house now. I should be there around 3:30 pm."

"Okay," I said. That was more than enough time.

Once I got off the phone with Marvin, I went to the kitchen; Mom and I just did our normal thing. We ate and talked about life. I noticed my mom was in a different space, in deep thought.

Young Kaz

I didn't know what to think of it. I would often drift off into space, but I just watched her and wondered what was going on in her head. I enjoyed talking with her, but most of our conversations were based on me and what I wanted in life, my morals, and my respect for myself. Even though we had a man in the household, she would still do her part as Mommy and Daddy. That's what I loved about this woman.

"Mommy, everything okay?" I had to ask. "You know you can talk to me about anything, right?"

"Yes, baby, I know. I'm okay."

"Alright!"

I had a little time on my hands to do my daily norm before Marvin came home. When he came in, that was when it started up— Marvin chasing her around the table, trying to get a kiss, and me watching my mom smile like a little girl. There were times when I helped Marvin out with catching her, but she would just let me catch her, and they would grab each other like love birds that just met. Sometimes, I would have to lock my door because I would barge in on them giggling and playing with each other, and they would stop and look at me, like, *Oh, you going to get some of this loving too.*

Both of them would chase me, but I ended that chase quickly with a nice quick dash right to my room, slamming the door behind me and locking them out. I just started recently engaging in the cat-and-mouse chase with them, which would end up in a pillow fight.

"Hey, Pops," I said. "Are you ready now?"

"Yeah, let me rest just a little bit. I think I just drained myself." I kicked back and watched Marvin lay on the couch, and my mom lay on his chest. I knew what was next. The TV popped on, and you heard him snoring not too long after. Both of them were out like lights.

I went inside my room to kick back myself. I popped the radio on, and what do you know, my jam was playing: "I Want to Rock With You" by Bobby Brown. I began singing the song while having my own little karaoke challenge.

I was having a good time. I enjoyed myself so much that I didn't recall looking at the door until the song "It's My Prerogative" came on. By then, I was a little sweaty and humping around the room, literally—yes, I lost myself. I came to reality quickly when Mom and Marvin started humping around in the room with me, laughing. I swear I had the coolest parents.

Rickey Dudley

Alright, already. Y'all get out!" I shoved them both out of my room. "Y'all have to go." I pushed them out as if they were stealing the show.

They sang as if they were in sync with one another: "It's my prerogative, and I can do what I want to do," they replied, laughing while leaving my room.

"I'm ready when you are," says Marvin.

I said, "Ok." I had to stop pretending to be Bobby Brown and get back to myself. I freshened up, and Marvin and I left to go to Target. As soon as we parked, we heard a commotion. One lady was yelling at someone because they had taken her parking spot. I watched Marvin, and he said, "Oh well, that has nothing to do with us," and kept moving.

If there was one thing I could say for a fact about Marvin, it was that he most definitely stayed in his own lane. We walked around, picking stuff out that Mom needed so she could cook for the week, and while doing so, I noticed they were hiring. Sure enough, I didn't have any plans in my life, so I thought, why not go for it? But then again, I would have to travel all the way here alone, which wouldn't work for me.

"What do you know, they're hiring? That would be a good look, Kaz. You can make some money," Marvin said.

"Yeah, sounds good, but getting back and forth would be a journey."

"Nah, I'll drive you until you get your license."

"License?" I said. "You need a license to work here?"

"No, silly. I mean, until you get your driver's license, I'm going to help you."

"Oh, that's great. When do we start?"

"We can start now. I'll show you once we get out of here."

We continued shopping, making sure we had everything that Mom wanted. I was ready to go the moment he said, "I'll show you how."

As we walked, I thought about driving around, listening to my music, and going places. It felt good for a moment, and then that was when the unthinkable happened. Over and over, it started playing in my mind; first, I heard the gunshot and then watched the body drop in slow motion. It went from that to back to the school, hearing Joy's screams and cries. "You know who did it, you motherfucker. You know!" No matter what I tried, I just couldn't block that memory out of my head...

"Hey, snap out of it, kid. You good?"

"Yeah, Pops. I'm good," I said. "I was just daydreaming."

"Yeah, you have been gone for a minute. Did you bring anything back with you?" he said, joking while laughing hysterically.

We finished getting all the stuff that Moms needed once again, but on our way out, Marvin suggested that I should go ask for an application. It was a good idea. I wasn't doing anything with myself, was out of school, and had nothing but time on my hands.

Young Kaz

Check this out. You can work for Target and see pretty women. You can also learn how to shop by watching people and, at the same time, put money in your pocket. That's some real-life lessons for you, kid. Oh, and did I mention pretty women, too?" We both laughed at the idea, but there was truth in it.

Marvin had this way of telling me what I needed in life, but not from a father's standpoint. It was more in a joking way. The way he explained it made perfect sense. I asked for an application, but I had to fill it out right then and there, and I did. Once I got back in the car, my lessons started.

"Ok, once you sit in the car, you put your seat belt on—that's very important for safety first. Second, you put the key in the ignition and turn it toward the right-side wheel of the car just enough to hear the engine roll over like this. Listen." He started the car, and I began thinking, *Ok, was there something I missed when he started it up the last time?* "Now you check your mirror's right side, left side, and your rear view. The side mirrors help you see on the sides. The rear view shows you what's behind you. For example, the Cops, Fire Trucks, and E.M.Ts." I watched every move that he made, trying to remember all of them. He drove away and said, "Okay, that's enough for now. Just watch me as we drive home. Pay attention to how I step on the gas and brakes. Also, look at the distance between me and the other cars when I stop."

As we came to a stop at the red light, I noticed this one light-skinned dude in army fatigue gear, but the colors were black and white. He was just staring at Marvin, that same stare that I received from Joy when she said she was going to kill me. Believe me, there was nothing cool about knowing someone wanted to kill you.

"Pop, why is that guy looking at you like that? The one with the army gear on, on your left side."

"Just tell me his every move without looking dead at him, ok? And by the way, laugh."

I couldn't understand why Marvin didn't want to look in this guy's direction. When the light turned green, I started to laugh as if I had heard a hilarious joke, looking at this strange dude from my peripheral vision. His stare was precise on Marvin. As we drove away, I looked at Marvin, and he didn't look worried, not one bit. "Hey, Pops, do you know that guy? He looked angry."

"Nah, I don't. Maybe he was looking at someone else."

"No way, Pops. He looked like he wanted blood. I know that stare," I explained. "That's the same way Joy stared at me when she said she was going to kill me.

Rickey Dudley

arvin looked at me and said, "Okay, champ, I get it." I noticed slight anger in his tone when he said, "I get it," so I changed the topic.

"I tell you what, Pops, I'll call this woman as soon as I get in the house."

"No way, champ! You have to play it cool. Don't look like a thirst bucket."

"But I am. I want that woman bad, Pops!" I motioned to my hands, forming a Coca-Cola bottle shape to describe her figure. We were both laughing when, suddenly, that laughing stopped abruptly. I randomly looked toward my right and saw a yellow and black car pulled up on the side, stopping at the red light. I saw the driver in army fatigue gear, but this one was red and white. Unbeknownst to me, there was that same dude in the army fatigue in black and white, looking in my direction. We locked eyes right after he began to yell, "Hell yeah, that's that motherfucker!"

I was so scared that I just slumped in the seat, telling Marvin to "Eat the light." Marvin looked in my direction and took off immediately. I felt uncomfortable with the memories of Joy coming back. For all I knew, this might've been her people out to get revenge. While riding like a bat out of hell, I took the liberty to check and see how far they were, but they didn't even give chase. "Pops, I'm sorry I got you caught in my mess, but I swear I don't know who those guys were. All I did was look and didn't do anything else, I swear."

"Don't worry. Just sit back and chill."

"I'm scared, Pops. I want to go home."

"We are going home, but not straight away. We're going to make a couple of turns so they don't find out where we live."

Marvin got on the phone, and on the other end, I could hear my mom's voice, but before she could start her usual, "Hey, baby!" Marvin cut her short, telling her, "Plans had changed."

The phone went silent for a second or two then, and I heard a different tone on my mom's end that I'd never heard before. "Get here when you get here," she replied.

When Marvin got off the phone, he told me to listen well. He explained how bad of a situation we all were in and who those guys were. By the time Marvin was done explaining, we were pulling up to the house. We walked in, and Marvin began speaking to Mom right away.

"I explained some things to him. I had no choice but the important part I left out for you to tell him." *Wait, there's more?* I thought to myself.

"Go to your room, baby, and get some sleep. It's nine o'clock. You've heard enough for now. We'll finish this tomorrow."

I went to my room as my mom insisted. I noticed all my things were packed: pictures, posters, and clothes. There it goes, that one memory I'd never forget. That light burgundy-brown blanket. That was Mom's signature way of saying for me to get rest because we were moving in the morning. I knew time was against me, but for some reason, I went straight to sleep.

Young Kaz

I quickly got to sleep, but just as quickly, Mom was shaking me awake, demanding I get up and dressed. Unbeknownst to her, I went to sleep in my clothes because I knew that when I got up, there would be nothing but movement at a fast pace—no breakfast, just getting things out of the house and into the car.

On our last trip to the car, heading out of the house to leave for good, Mom opened the door, and there was a strange man out front with a sign that said, "Fuck you, bitch." My mom was so angry. She cursed at him while swinging at his face to give him that one-hitter quitter.

He had this strange grin on his face as if he'd hit the jackpot, leaning on that same black and yellow car. Before I could say a word, I heard a loud blast and felt what I thought were raindrops on the left side of my face. I looked to my left at where my mom was to see where the wetness came from. She was falling down in slow motion, and I then caught sight of the gunshot wound, which had caught us off guard.

I felt paralyzed. I looked at the guy who shot my mom in the eye, and in slow motion, he aimed the gun at me. Before he could get a precise aim, his brain was blown out from his right side by Marvin. The shot woke me from the state of shock that I was in, and

I turned toward the guy holding the sign. He drew out his gun, shooting while trying to get away, but Marvin was able to catch him in the head as well before taking two shots himself.

I wanted to cry, but I couldn't because my lungs felt tight inside. I was falling to the ground, gasping for air while trying to reach out to Marvin and my mom, who were lying still on the floor. I made one attempt to crawl to them before I blacked out.

THE END